CAMERON JUDD

REVENGE ON SHADOW TRAIL

POCKET STAR BOOKS

NEW YORK   LONDON   TORONTO   SYDNEY   SINGAPORE

This book is a work of fiction. Names, characters, places and incidents are products of the author's imagination or are used fictitiously. Any resemblance to actual events or locales or persons, living or dead, is entirely coincidental.

An *Original* Publication of POCKET BOOKS

A Pocket Star Book published by
POCKET BOOKS, a division of Simon & Schuster, Inc.
1230 Avenue of the Americas, New York, NY 10020

Copyright © 2003 by Cameron Judd

ISBN: 0-7434-5709-9

First Pocket Books printing October 2003

10 9 8 7 6 5 4 3 2 1

POCKET STAR BOOKS and colophon are registered trademarks of Simon & Schuster, Inc.

Front cover illustration by Bruce Emmett

Manufactured in the United States of America

For information regarding special discounts for bulk purchases, please contact Simon & Schuster Special Sales at 1-800-456-6798 or business@simonandschuster.com

MOTHER AND CHILD

Liam stared at the woman hiding beneath his bed. Long hair, auburn, with long and seemingly natural curls. Face pale, unblemished, eyes brown and deep. She was beauty incarnate . . . overtaken by terror. The fear in her expression was palpable.

"Who is after you, and why?" Liam asked.

A click at the window, ever so faint, metal brushing glass. . . .

Liam remembered the man on the porch. At the window now. That noise—a pistol barrel, grazing the window?

"Oh, God preserve me, and God preserve my poor, unborn child!" the girl said in a sharp and very Irish-inflected whisper, and dropped to the floor, huddling beside the bed.

Swearing beneath his breath, Liam hurried to the window and defiantly threw open the curtain. A young man, thin and raggedly whiskered, leaped back in surprise, a pistol in his hand. . . .

PRAISE FOR THE WESTERN FICTION OF CAMERON JUDD

"*The Overmountain Men* is a story of courage, blood-shed, and a way of life that we cannot even imagine. Be sure to get your copy. You won't be able to put it down."

—*Valdosta Daily Times* (GA)

Also by Cameron Judd

SHOOTOUT IN DODGE CITY

REVENGE
ON SHADOW TRAIL

PROLOGUE

"Let me tell you about the first man I killed," said the man with the flourishing mustache. He had an easy smile and a head of sandy hair that had remained with him even though his youth was long behind. But his eyes were cold as frost as he stared at the young man to whom he spoke.

"He was a famous one. Quite the gunfighter. It made my reputation the moment I dropped him. Three bullets. Killed him instantly . . . sorry, friend, but it won't be as fast for you as it was for old-Colonel Bishop. You've heard of Colonel Bishop, no doubt."

The young man, bound at the wrists with his hands behind his back, turned and spat at the mustached man. He missed, and the big man laughed.

The smaller, weasely fellow with them didn't laugh. He yanked hard on the rope that encircled the bound young man's neck and pulled him completely off his feet. The young man landed on his side in the Missouri dirt.

"Show some respect to your elders and betters!" the weaselly man said, jerking the rope again and kicking at the fallen man.

The man with the mustache laughed again, leaned over, and spat onto the face of the bound young man. "There, Mr. Irishman, that's how you spit! You missed me by a good three feet, and I got you right in the eye! Then, I always hit my targets, as you'll see again in a few minutes. Come on, now, get on your feet. We're nearly to your final destination."

The young man swore at his captors, who leaned above him, their forms limned against a sky that still showed the last faint ghosts of daylight.

"You've got spirit, I'll grant you that," the mustached man said. "Even Maxwell said that. With some admiration in his voice, I might add. Of course, right after that he told me to get rid of you. Too bad for you, eh?"

"If Maxwell was half a man, he'd face me himself, not send some hired gunny too big a fool to make a living any other way than killing people for hire."

"Umm umm umm!" the other said, shaking his head slowly. "You ain't the brightest, Irishman! Here I am, a man who can kill you fast and painless or slow and painful, and you're talking all antagonistic! Don't you want a fast and easy death, son?"

2

The young man slowly came to his feet, a task made more difficult by his bonds.

"I know your kind, Coldwell. You enjoy what you do. You'd not show me mercy no matter what I said or didn't say. And I'm not going to just roll over and let you kill me without putting up whatever fight I can. Even if all I can do is spit in your face."

"Big talk, but look at him shaking!" chortled the weaselly one.

"He ought to shake. He'll be in hell in five minutes. He can say hello to Colonel Bishop there. Speaking of him, let me finish my story, Irishman. It's got some similarities to yours. I was hired to kill Colonel Bishop by a man of means who didn't like the fact Bishop was dallying with his wife . . . just like you dallied with Mr. Maxwell's young lady."

"She's not his young lady. She's the woman I'm going to marry! She despises Maxwell . . . she does what she does because he's forced her to it!"

"Hear that, Sam? He thinks he's going to a wedding! A funeral is more like it, friend. Not that you'll get one, rotting away out here on the plains."

Coldwell suddenly kicked the bound man, making him fall down on one knee. His false joviality was gone all at once. "Listen to me, you Irish piece of dung, I'm tired of your mouth and backtalk. You crossed the wrong man when you crossed Crane Maxwell, and he's hired me to do a job for him because of it. Ain't nothing personal. Just a job. But dammit, it's about to get personal! I don't like you, Irishman!"

"You can go to hell."

"Uh-uh. You do it." Coldwell looked around. "Looks like as good a place as any, Sam. Nobody around, probably nobody close enough even to hear the shot. Let's go ahead and take care of it right now."

"Make him run!" Sam said, giggling now. "Moon's out enough . . . we'll make some sport of it!"

"Not a bad notion, Sam. Take the rope from around his neck."

"You'd backshoot a tied-up, unarmed man?"

"Sure would, pilgrim. I'll do it and sleep like a sweet Irish bairn, I will." He smiled slowly, face illuminated by the moonlight. His hand crept to his pistol. "Run, Irishman. Run hard! I'm giving you a chance to get away . . . but you'll not get far."

"I'll not turn my back to you. If you want to kill me, have the gravel to do it to my face!"

"It ain't me who wants to kill you. It's Crane Maxwell. You should have stayed away from the girl, I tell you."

"He has no right to her. He's a married man."

"A man with his money has the right to whatever and whoever he wants. What do you want with a whore like her, anyway?"

4

Coldwell clicked back the hammer of his pistol and aimed it at the young man. "Run, Irishman. Now."

Though his hands were tied, though there was no hope of success, the young man lunged at Coldwell, kicking, elbowing, butting with his head. Coldwell took a ram right in the forehead and staggered back. Still the young man came on.

Sam, startled, fumbled for his own pistol, but Coldwell moved faster. Sidestepping away from his foe, he raised his pistol and fired. The blast echoed across the Missouri flatlands, and the flash burned for a moment as brightly as day.

The young man's body kicked back as if struck by a hammer. His feet came out from beneath him, and he landed on his back, eyes wide-open and staring at the moon. They closed, halfway, and he let out a long, slow breath.

And then all was quiet.

1

Joseph Carrigan saw the sign through the black murk of a smoke-stained passenger train window and the even blacker murk of waning sleep. It flitted through the corner of his vision as the train rolled past one more nameless town. His eyes opened wider, and he sat up quickly.

His brother Liam was slouched back on the benchlike seat, hat tilted down over his nose, arms folded across his chest, body trembling ever so slightly from the rumbling vibration of the train. He breathed evenly, his lips moving a little with every inhalation.

"Did you see it?" Joseph said.

Liam grunted softly.

"Liam! Did you see it?" Joseph rubbed his hand across his face and kicked his brother lightly with the scuffed toe of his boot.

Liam sat up, dropping his hat, and glared at

Joseph. With four days of stubble on his face, hair too long uncut, and an expression at the moment quite fearsome, he would have been an intimidating sight to anyone but his own brother.

"Did you just kick me?" Liam demanded.

"Did you see that sign? Out the window?"

"I was asleep. I didn't see anything."

"Well, I saw it. 'Pat Carrigan.' It was written right there on a sign. Big red letters. I swear!"

Liam swiped his hand down his face and yawned. "Now, what? Say that again."

"We passed through a town, just a moment ago. I looked out the window and saw a sign with the name of Patrick Carrigan on it."

Liam yawned and scratched at his stubble and gave his head a fog-clearing shake. "I need coffee."

Joseph turned and raised his window, sticking his head out to look back toward the little town they'd passed through. But the train had moved too far and was rounding a gentle turn. He pulled his head back inside and closed the window.

"Good Lord, Joseph, you let all kinds of soot and smoke in when you open that window. Leave it shut!"

"I'm telling you, Liam, there was a sign back there."

"Maybe there was. Maybe there wasn't. We're past it now, so we can't tell. Now let me go back to sleep."

"Is that all you want to do? Sleep?"

"No. I like to drink and play cards and carouse with pretty women, too. Sleep's not even on the top of the list."

Joseph fidgeted. "We've got to go back. We've got to see about that sign."

"Dammit, Joseph, we're going to Montana. We're going to find Uncle Patrick. In Montana. Not here."

"We don't know for sure. I only know what I saw."

"You saw nothing. You dreamed it. Now go back to sleep and let me do the same!"

"Liam, I swear, I don't know sometimes why I even stay around you! You're so blasted cocky confident that you know everything, all the time! You apparently even can tell me what I did and didn't see!"

Liam swore and shifted his position, turning his left shoulder toward his brother and trying to find a comfortable resting posture on the hard seat. Joseph stared at him a minute or so, then looked back out the window again.

Liam began to snore softly.

"I know what I saw," Joseph said.

Liam opened his eyes, turned to glare at Joseph, then swore loudly. A woman passing on the aisle looked at him in horror.

"Pardon my brother, ma'am," Joseph said. "He's not a good man."

Liam swore again. The woman hurried on.

Liam's eyes were fiery, but his voice was quieter

when he spoke. "You know, Joseph, sometimes it truly is hard to put up with you. You have a way of just draining the folks who are around you. All righteous and wanting to decide everything for everybody else all the time . . . just drains a soul away, being around you."

"Maybe when we get to Montana, you won't have to be around me anymore. Maybe I'll take up with Patrick and be a rancher, and you can move on and be a traveling gambler and womanizer."

"Sounds better than you know."

Joseph opened his mouth to retort but held himself back. He looked out the window and said nothing for nearly a minute. At last he did speak.

"I saw that sign, Liam. I think we need to go back and look at it."

"Shut up and give me some peace."

"Do you even want to find Uncle Patrick?"

"Why wouldn't I want to find him?"

"Because you believe, sometimes at least, that it's pointless. That the only reason we're trying to find him at all is that we can't seem to make a success of ourselves on our own."

"So you can read my mind now?"

"Am I wrong?"

"Of course you're wrong. You're always wrong."

"There's no point in talking to you about anything, I guess."

"You're right. There's not. So why don't you just shut up for a spell, and give me some peace?"

Ten minutes later, as Joseph was lost in thought, gazing out the dirty window, Liam abruptly sat up and spoke again. His manner was different now.

"Was it a sign on a building?" he asked.

Joseph was actually startled by the sudden intrusion of his brother's voice. "No. On the ground, but leaned up enough to read. There was rubbish around it . . . and a fire. Someone burning trash, I think. It's not a clear picture in my mind . . . mostly an impression. I was half-asleep when I saw it."

"Well, then, I'd say you dreamed it. We're heading to Montana to find Patrick Carrigan, you've got that on your mind, and so you dreamed you saw his name on a sign."

Joseph pondered the possibility. "No . . . I saw it, Liam. 'Pat Carrigan.' I'm sure."

Liam rubbed the sleep from his eyes and leaned back, staring at the ceiling of the rumbling passenger car. "Could it really be *our* Pat Carrigan?"

"Maybe."

Liam pulled the corpse of a half-smoked cigar from his vest pocket and set about resurrecting it. Straightening it, caressing it, shaping it gently, he fired a match and lit up, filling the cubicle with acrid smoke. He blew a smoke ring and watched it dissolve.

11

"So maybe we should get off the next stop and go back, like you said," he said. "What town was that?"

"I don't know. A small place. A few stores, and I saw a saloon."

"Ah! Indeed we should go back!"

"Why the change of heart?"

"You know me, Joseph. I always give in to your way in the end. It makes life easier in the long run and helps give you the notion that you actually do have good sense instead of being the fool you really are."

"You're very kind to me, brother."

"Don't mention it."

"Just think, Liam . . . what if Uncle Patrick himself is back there? Maybe he lives in that town. Maybe he has a store, or ran for mayor. Maybe that was him burning the rubbish."

Liam sent out another toxic cloud of smoke, then settled the cigar in the corner of his mouth. "You're surmising a mighty lot from one glimpse of a sign, my brother. I still think you may have dreamed it."

"I don't think so."

"We'll go back, then. We'll get off at the next stop, get the horses out of the stable car, and go back to see. While we're there, we may as well visit that saloon."

"Is that a life goal of yours, Liam? To visit every saloon west of the Mississippi?"

"I could think of lesser ambitions."

Liam lay back again, the stinking cigar clamped between his teeth. He puffed it a few times, but as he began to doze off again, let it go cold. Joseph watched him sleep for a while, then leaned over and began to nap himself.

Sometime later, the train jolted violently. Joseph opened his eyes wide and saw Liam flung from his seat, thrown into the air like a doll stuffed with straw. Joseph himself followed less than a moment later, slamming his head hard against the ceiling, everything going brilliant white, then black. He fell back on the seat with his body twisted to one side and his left hand beneath him, taking the brunt of his weight on three fingers.

Then he tumbled. He caught a glimpse of Liam's form moving past him, in the air. The cigar was still clamped in Liam's mouth, and Joseph would forever after wonder why such a small detail would stand out to him in the midst of a train crash.

Joseph landed on the same hand as before. Pain stabbed through his fingers, and he blacked out again, still in motion.

"This one's alive," said the man who loomed above Joseph. "Just stunned, I think. Hey, there, friend, is your hand hurting?"

"Yes," Joseph said. His left hand was lying across

his belly. When he touched it with his right hand, it made him wince.

"I don't think you've broke no bones. Your fingers ain't crooked or nothing. The doc will get to you eventually. Just be patient, and you'll be a patient." He paused, then laughed. "You hear that? I made kind of a joke or such there, and wasn't even trying. Just be patient, and you'll be a patient! Ha!"

"My brother . . . is he all right?"

"I don't know him, sir. Was he on this train?"

"Yes."

"We ain't detected no one killed, and the injuries seem fairly light, considering how bad it could have been. So I'd say he's fine."

"We derailed?"

"You sure did. Bad stretch of track. A whole section of rail worked so loose it might as well not have been there at all. Got to go, friend. Got to look at some other folks." The man's looming form moved away, leaving Joseph staring up at the sky.

He lay still about a minute, then decided to rise. Joseph pushed up with his good hand and looked around. Most of the train was off the track, lying jumbled up like a child's tossed-away toy. Heavy steam and hissing noises emanated from the overturned locomotive; railroad men moved around the great and injured beast of iron with earnest expressions.

14

Everything looked hellish. The locomotive lay on its side, smoking. Railroad cars were twisted and splintered; cargo was strewn on the ground. The air was heavy with a stench of reeking smoke.

People were all about, both former passengers of the train and residents of the nearby town. Boys and dogs weaved through the mix, having a fine time in all the excitement as dogs and boys always do. The air was rich with a babble of voices, some talking quietly, some loudly, some weeping and others laughing, the railroad men barking official-sounding orders at one another. A burly man with a homemade pewter badge on his shirt lumbered by, bushy brows lowered into a burning scowl, and scolded one of the playful boys. "You there, Jimmy! Get that dog out of here! We got hurt folks!"

Joseph looked for Liam and spotted him almost immediately, to his relief. Liam was kneeling beside a crying young woman, giving her comfort and gentle words. She was quite pretty; Joseph had noticed her when they boarded the train. Her strawberry blond hair, which had been piled into a most impressive and gravity-defying coif, was now a ruined mess about her shoulders. Liam's expression as he dealt with her was as earnest as that of a priest at a parishioner's deathbed. His hand tenderly patting the young woman's shoulder. Liam glanced up. His eye caught Joseph's, and he gave a quick wink and grin.

Joseph stood slowly, checking himself out for injury as he did so. So far he seemed fine other than his hand, which throbbed with pain.

Liam appeared at his side. Joseph looked at him wryly. "Liam, it's a comfort and blessing to have a brother who shows such dedication to his kin. I'm lying senseless on the ground, could be dead for all you know, and you're over there talking up some weeping little wilted flower with a pretty face."

"Hey, don't scold me. I knew you were all right. I talked to you about it. Don't you remember?"

"You never talked to me."

"I did indeed! You sounded addled, but you told me you were fine, except for your fingers, and I told you that a doctor was coming around and would fix you up. You remember, surely."

"I don't."

"Then I guess you were more addled than I thought. I made sure you were fine, then went over to do my duty as a good Christian Irishman for that lovely young woman. Jennifer Jacques. Pretty name, huh? Kind of like poetry. The poor thing took quite a knock on the forehead, but I think she'll be fine, if she receives enough good manly comfort. She's traveling alone. And don't she look good with her hair all messed up that way! Women always look better that way, but you try to tell them that and they never believe you."

"I'm curious, Liam. If this is all pure-hearted charity on your part, why didn't you help out that poor old gray-haired grandmother over yonder? She looks worse off than poor little Jennifer."

"Hey, I can't bear all the responsibilities around here alone, can I? That one's yours to help."

"My hand hurts, Liam."

"You probably need it splinted."

"Then help me find something to splint it with."

"Keep your shirt on. That man kneeling over that fellow there is a doctor. He'll do a better job of splinting than I ever could. Excuse me now. I need to get back to Jennifer."

2

When Joseph saw the ruins of the stable car, he marveled that any of the horses had survived. But all had, save one old gelding that was so old that the owner speculated it had dropped dead from sheer fright when the train derailed.

The horses were now rounded up and penned in a makeshift rope corral. Saddles and other such gear rescued from the ruined stable car were laid out on the ground and under guard by a couple of young, strapping men apparently deputized for that job by the local sheriff, the big man with the perpetual scowl and pewter badge.

A man leaned against a nearby wagon, smoking and watching the hubbub. His clean clothing marked him as a local resident rather than a victim of the crash. Joseph approached him.

"Good day, sir," he said, touching his hat. "Might I ask you the name of the town just ahead?" Joseph nodded toward the northwest and the little railroad stop village visible there.

"That's Culpepperville."

"And the town back down the track?"

"That would be Hooper."

"How far back is it?"

"Oh, seven, eight miles." The man eyed Joseph's hand, which by now had been splinted and bandaged by the harried doctor. "You hurt bad, friend?"

"One cracked finger and two sprained ones. Nothing serious."

The man wandered off, and Joseph stared back down the track. An eight-mile ride. Should he go? The last information the Carrigan brothers had received indicated that the Patrick Carrigan they sought was more likely in Montana, and so it was to Montana they'd been bound. Was it worth backtracking?

Joseph was pondering all this when Liam rejoined him.

"Glad to see the horses made it through. Are you thinking about riding back to investigate that sign?"

"I am."

"How far?"

"Eight miles or so."

"Uh . . . you mind making the ride alone?"

"Why alone? On the train you said we'd both go back."

"Things have changed. I'm to accompany the lovely Jennifer to dinner this evening in whatever cafe we can find in that little town up yonder. She needs more comforting."

"I should have known. Yeah, I can go alone. I believe I'm supposed to. That sign had to be a sign."

"Most signs are."

"You know what I mean. Guidance. A portent. I see the sign, then, just a few miles up the track, we derail and crash so that suddenly I have the opportunity to go back and investigate. It can't be coincidence."

"Nothing is ever coincidence to you. You could find divine guidance in the route a roach takes across the parlor floor. And remember, this may not even be the right Patrick Carrigan."

"But what if it is? It's not the kind of name you'll run into just anywhere. It's not Joe Smith or John Jones."

"Why, there's probably hundreds of Pat Carrigans in this nation. There's a lot of Irish in America."

"Still, I'm going back."

"Fine. But forget this 'portent' nonsense. I've got some trouble with the notion that God Almighty derailed a train just to make it easy for you to ride eight miles to gander at some sign."

"Actually, Liam, I was thinking that maybe He derailed that train so you could meet Jennifer Jacques."

Liam's brows went up. "Hmm. Good point, Joseph. Very deep. So I guess it's all the more my moral duty to take good care of her."

"Then go take care of her. But I suggest you be a gentleman, Liam. She looks like a decent woman, not one of the saloon harlots you usually consort with. She's got an air of class about her, and I doubt she'd put up with any nonsense."

"I'll be a gentleman, thank you, Reverend Morality."

"I'll see you tomorrow, then. I'll find a room in Hooper and come back in the morning."

"What if you can't find a room?"

"Then I'll sleep under somebody's porch."

"The railroad's lodging everybody free in hotels right here, because of the crash. A free supper, too, and breakfast come morning. You're missing free lodging and food by going back."

"Then I'll miss them. I truly do believe I'm supposed to do this."

"Suit yourself, brother."

The anticipated eight miles turned out to be ten. By the time Joseph reached Hooper, the sky was beginning to darken, the breeze was growing cool, and he was hungry and nearly convinced that he was as muddleheaded a fool as Liam ever thought him to

21

be. If he'd stayed in Culpepperville, he'd be enjoying a delicious free supper about now and anticipating a peaceful rest in a good hotel bed.

Looking at the dismal little village of Hooper, he couldn't begin to guess where he'd sleep. He saw nothing that was obviously a hotel. The saloon was lively, though, and there were rooms on its second floor. Maybe those were for rent.

He rode his weary horse slowly around the little settlement, which clearly owed its existence to the railroad and the scattered ranches in the area. It was a foul and dirty-looking place, one that seemed old though it couldn't really be so in a world as young as the opening American West.

By the last light of day he tracked down the area where he'd spotted the sign. It was a back lot of a general mercantile store, a big, rambling building that sagged at odd places. Joseph found the remnants of the fire he'd seen burning when the train passed. It still smoked and smoldered, red coals twinkling and glowing in the dimming light. The rubbish heap was now almost entirely gone. There was no sign.

Joseph felt deflated. All this long ride, and now the very piece of potential evidence he sought was burned up, if it had existed at all. He should have stayed put in Culpepperville.

No chance for that now. Before he'd left, the railroad had informed the former passengers that another train would arrive to continue them on their journey at ten the next morning. So Joseph needed to find supper, a bed, and a place to feed and stable his weary horse so he could be up early in the morning and back off to Culpepperville in time to avoid missing the new train.

He rode up to the town's main street. The saloon, called the Saddlehorn, was the only obvious place to go. Light spilled out its open door, and three horses were tied at the hitching rail before it. Joseph heard the faint twang of gut guitar strings playing a Mexican song.

All up and down the rest of the street, nothing but dark doorways, mostly dark windows, except for the windows of the few residences. One man sat in a rocker on the porch of what was apparently his home. His body was thin and old; the rocker barely moved.

Yes, sir, a lively place this was. It might prove to be a long night.

Joseph tied his horse at the rail in front of the saloon and entered. An old, extraordinarily thin Mexican man was the guitarist. Joseph watched his bony fingers fly over the strings and frets. Not bad. Joseph had always wished he could be a musician, but never had the opportunity to learn.

Stomach rumbling suddenly, Joseph headed for the bar. The barkeep was one of those grown men who still looks like a boy, but his voice was sonorous and operatic. "What for you this fine evening, sir?"

"I'm looking for food," Joseph said. "Or do you serve only liquor?"

"We have a limited but outstanding selection of fine victuals," the young man said almost haughtily, as if this were a fine French eatery worthy of Boston or New York.

"Steak?"

"Indeed."

"Potatoes?"

"Not always, but you're in luck today."

"Biscuits?"

"Baked fresh every morning by my own dear mother. And that, sir, is pretty much the menu."

"I'll take a steak, potato with butter, and all the biscuits you can load in a basket. And a beer to wash it down."

"Indeed. We'll get that food cooked as quick as we can."

The beer Joseph didn't have to wait for. He carried it back to a table in the corner and sat down, wondering why he'd bought it. He almost never drank; the last time had been one night in Dodge City when he and Liam sneaked some liquor from the desk of a liveryman Joseph was working for at the time. Liam was the drinker of the family, more than making up for what Joseph declined to imbibe.

Joseph sipped the beer and looked around at the mostly somnolent occupants of the establishment. The Mexican finished one song and began another; Joseph chuckled as he recognized a Stephen Foster tune given a south-of-the-border flavor.

The rest of the patrons showed little interest in Joseph. In fact, they showed little interest in anything, including their drinks. Joseph wondered just how dull a town could be. If Liam were there, he'd be ready to hang himself from boredom within an hour. Or, he'd find a way to liven things up.

The scent of cooking steak filled the saloon. Soon the aroma of a baking potato joined it, and Joseph's stomach rumbled again, loudly. He sipped the beer and, being unaccustomed to much alcohol, quickly felt a warmth fill his stomach and a general sense of contentment spread through his being. He was tired, had failed to find that sign he'd ridden ten miles to investigate, and had no notion about where he'd spend the night. But at least he'd have a good supper. Maybe he'd finish it off with a second beer for dessert.

The guitarist broke a string and retired to the bar. Joseph's meal arrived, and he set in eagerly but slowly. He had a long and boring night ahead. No reason to rush into it. Besides, it wasn't easy to cut steak with splinted fingers.

Joseph was halfway through his meal when the

boyish barkeep came around with a rag, swiping down the tabletops.

"How's the steak?" he asked Joseph.

"Excellent. But there's one thing I need: a little information, if you have it."

"What's that, sir?"

"I heard a rumor there might be a relative of mine in town here. Fellow name of Carrigan. Patrick Carrigan. Some might call him Pat."

Silence. And it lingered just a moment too long, Joseph thought. Then the barkeep gave a thoughtful squint, one brow arched. "Carrigan. No, no. Don't recall knowing nobody by that name. And I know most folks all around here."

"Maybe he was a visitor to town, then," Joseph suggested. "A drummer maybe. Somebody who would have a sign with his name on it, because I caught a glimpse of such a sign today, being burned with some rubbish over near the railroad track."

"Don't know any Carrigan, sir. Sorry."

Joseph nodded and went back to his meal, trying to decide if he was being lied to. Eventually he persuaded himself that his imagination was running amuck, and considered again Liam's theory that he had simply dreamed up the sign. Perhaps he'd been foolish to ride a full ten miles for the sake of nothing more than a fleeting visual impression through a dirty train window.

Finishing at last, Joseph went to the bar and paid the young barkeep for his meal. "Is there a hotel in town?" he asked.

"Well, not really. We had one here, a right good one, but dang if it didn't burn down recently. They just got the rubble from it cleaned up recently . . . they burned the last of it today, in fact. That's probably the rubbish you saw being burned."

"Out behind the mercantile?"

"Yep. Jim Taylor's boy, Mark, would have been the one burning it. He's a little slow in the head. Got dropped when he was little. He likes to burn things. You ask me, I think he might have burned the hotel. But I'll deny saying that if asked."

"Could this boy tell me if there in fact was a sign with the name of Pat Carrigan on it?"

"Not likely. He can't read his own name. If there was such a sign, he'd never be able to tell you what it said."

"Who owned the hotel, then? Maybe he'd know."

"He might."

"Where would I find him?"

"That'll be the trick, sir. He moved off to Kansas last week."

Joseph gave up. "All right, then. Then let me ask you if there is a stable in town where I could leave my horse for the night."

"The only livery was beside the hotel. Sparks hit it, and it burned, too. Sorry."

"Yeah."

He left the saloon. Nothing remained now of the daylight. Leading his horse down the street, he turned down a side alley and began exploring the back lots and side avenues, what few there were in so small a place.

Eventually he stumbled upon the site where the hotel had apparently stood. A foundation and chimney remained, and a few charred timbers. And over to the side, half a stable, charred and black—but the part still standing looked relatively sturdy. There was room there for his horse. Maybe he could even bed down in there himself.

The stench of burned wood, however, was far too strong for human endurance. The horse would spend the night in there alone. Joseph put it in the only remaining stall, hung the saddle and bridle over the stall's side, and fed the horse from a small supply of feed he'd brought with him.

Taking his rolled blankets, he exited the ruined stable in search of a place to sleep. He spotted a dark little unpainted house, hardly more than a shack, no lights burning inside. Adjacent to it was a woodshed with a door ajar. He headed for the woodshed.

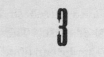

3

Joseph was about to enter the shed when the smell of cigar smoke reached his nose. A faint dot of red flared beside the shack like a floating willow wisp, and a gravelly, rich voice said, "Good evening, sir."

Startled, Joseph turned. A man was seated in a straight-backed chair over beside the shack. The chair was tilted back against the wall. Against the dark and shadowed wall Joseph had initially spotted neither chair nor man.

"Good evening," Joseph said.

"Fine night, ain't it, sir!" observed the man in the chair. From his voice, Joseph detected the speaker was a black man.

"Indeed."

"I believe you must be looking for a place to sleep, sir."

"The truth is . . . yes. I saw the shed, and thought perhaps it would be no harm to anyone if—"

"No need to explain yourself, sir. I've spent many a night in many a shed myself. There's times a man has to take what shelter he can find." The chair tilted forward, and the man came to his feet and advanced to Joseph. He was stooped and old, small of frame, his head covered with thick but very gray curling hair.

"My name's Plunker. Plunker Freeman. This here's my house, and that there's my woodshed."

Joseph extended his hand. Plunker Freeman hesitated before he shook it. Joseph took no offense. For a white man to extend a hand to a black one was not common and no doubt threw Plunker a little off-balance.

"Pleased to meet you, Mr. Freeman. I apologize for intruding onto your property. When I saw there were no lights in your house, I thought perhaps it was not occupied."

"I just ain't been inside to light a lamp yet this evening, sir. Been enjoying this fine evening and smoking my cigar. That's my sitting place there, right in that chair, up against the wall. I welcome in the night there most the time."

Freeman had a friendly, pleasant manner that put Joseph at ease. "My name's Joseph," he said. "I'm passing through town and didn't know the hotel had burned down."

"Yes, sir. Quite a fire that was. I watched her burn

right to the ground. They saved half the stable, but there wasn't much point to that. They'll have to tear it down anyway. Should have let the fire have it."

"I've got a horse in there right now."

"Should be safe enough. You got anything to feed that horse?"

"Yes. It's already taken care of."

"And yourself, sir?"

"I ate at the saloon. A steak."

"Yes, sir. Fine. But have you had any good coffee today? I was thinking of making me up a potful. And coffee's always better shared."

Freeman was obviously determined to be hospitable. Joseph was glad to accept. "I'd be pleased, Mr. Freeman."

"Just call me Plunker, sir. Just old Plunker. That's me. Just plain old Plunker to one and all. I surely ain't used to being called 'Mister.'"

"Do you mind if I sleep in your shed, Plunker?"

"Not at all, Mr. Joseph. But if you'd rather, you're welcome to roll out your blankets inside my house. I see you've got a hurt hand. I'll not have no injured man staying in my shed when he can have the shelter of a real house. Unless you'd rather have the shed, of course."

"Are you always so kind to strangers?"

"I try to be, sir. 'Specially to them I sense I can trust. I've got a feel for such things, and I ain't been wrong yet. Now, if you'll come on in, we'll get us a lamp or two lit and set that coffee to boiling. Night's starting to get a nippy feel to it, and these old bones don't bear the cold the way they used to."

The coffee, boiled with an egg mixed with the grounds like cattle drive cooks typically made it, was one of the most satisfying beverages Joseph had enjoyed in months. He sat on Plunker Freeman's only padded chair—Plunker had insisted on it—and sipped the strong brew from a thick crockery cup with a broken handle. His blankets were already spread before the fireplace, where Plunker had built a small fire just the right intensity to knock the chill off the evening but not overheat the room.

Plunker produced a small blue flask from somewhere and added some of its contents to his coffee. He offered some to Joseph, but Joseph declined. Joseph had just finished outlining his and Liam's recent history—his own temporary stint as a town deputy in Dodge City, Kansas, and Liam's work there in a wagon shop. They'd left Dodge intending to go straight to Montana, but had done a small favor for a generously disposed man of means who repaid the kindness by hiring them to help build a couple of barns on some of his Missouri ranch property. They'd accepted the offer and made an eastward detour, worked for him a few weeks, and earned some decent traveling money. Now they were back on track again, so to speak, their journey to Montana resumed.

"Let me ask you something, Plunker," Joseph said. "I came to town this evening because earlier today, passing by on the train, I caught a glimpse of a sign being burned with a pile of rubbish. It had a name on it that intrigued me. Patrick Carrigan."

Plunker's cup froze halfway to his lips. He stared at Joseph like he'd just changed to someone else.

The cup lowered. "Why you interested in that name?"

"Because I've got an uncle by that name. An uncle I've never known. My brother and I have been searching for him. So when I saw that sign . . ."

"Wasn't your uncle. Not this Patrick Carrigan."

"How do you know?"

"Too young. Just a young man."

Joseph nodded, disappointed. "Well, I guess I've rode quite a few miles and imposed on you for nothing."

"Ain't no imposition."

"Tell me, Plunker, why did you freeze up like that when I mentioned Patrick Carrigan's name?"

"I guess because I felt so bad for the poor boy. He come to a bad end, sir. That's the story, anyway."

"What kind of bad end?"

"Don't really know, sir. All I've heard is gossip. But

the talk is this young fellow had bad people after him. He shows up here in town with his sign and his boxing gear and heads down to the saloon, looking for a fight. And he got his fight, three of them, matter of fact, and won them all."

"He's a prizefighter?"

"He'd take on any comer, and he was nothing to be trifled with. Muscle from ankle to neck. Solid as stone. But they say he found some trouble that he wasn't strong enough to whip."

"What kind of trouble?"

"The rumor is, somebody took him out of the hotel at gunpoint and out onto the flatlands somewhere. He never come back."

"They killed him?"

"That's the general belief, sir. That's the general belief."

"Why? Just because he won some fights?"

"I truly don't know. Nobody knows. But the feeling is that the young man came to town with trouble already following him, and it was here that it finally caught up with him. Maybe he owed money, maybe he'd done something to make somebody mad he shouldn't have made mad. His things remained behind, his clothes, the rope he used to string up a boxing ring, that sign of his . . . had to be the same one you saw, sir. But he was gone. Never come back. They put his things into storage and waited for him to return for them, but he never done it. Then when the hotel burned, it all burned up with it. Except the sign, I guess, if you seen it today."

"Well, even the sign is burned up now."

"It's a sad tale." Plunker paused. "But I admit I can't make myself feel as bad about it as I should. Not with them clothes he wore."

"What do you mean?"

Plunker hesitated. "Sir, I said too much when I said that. Never mind my foolish chattering."

"You've roused my curiosity, Plunker. What about his clothes offended you?"

"I fear to answer, sir, because I don't know what your side was in the late war."

"I fought for the Union."

Relief washed over Plunker's face. "Then I can tell you: Young Carrigan wore a Rebel uniform, or part of one. He called himself the Irish Rebel. I didn't much like that gray uniform. Reminded me of the times of the war."

"I can understand that. A gray uniform might make me a touch nervous myself. I've been shot at by many a man in gray."

"I admire your kind of soldier, sir. I come to love Mr. Lincoln's soldiers back in them hard old days. I lived in Carolina during the war, and more than once me and my sister, God rest her, we helped hide Mr. Lincoln's soldiers when they was on the run. We hid out some who had busted free from Rebel prison camps and was trying to get back to safe country. There was others who had just got separated from their units and needed to hide out until they could get back where they needed to be. And plenty more were just plain civilian folks who favored the Union and was trying to get out of Tennessee and such places, and make their way north to join the blue army. We helped many such, we did."

"On behalf of myself and all others who fought for the Union, I thank you, Mr. Freeman . . . Plunker."

"Do you like my name, sir? Freeman, I mean."

"A fine name."

"I took it on myself, when the war ended. Free-man. Free-man. It was how I celebrated the victory, taking on the name of Freeman."

Joseph raised his mug. "Here's to Plunker Freeman, a free man."

"Thank you, sir." With a broad grin, Plunker raised his own coffee cup, and they drank in tandem.

A few moments of silence followed. Plunker sipped his spiked coffee. Joseph stared at the fire, and despite the strong coffee he was drinking, felt sleepy. He looked forward to settling down in his blankets. Tomorrow would be an early morning.

Plunker and Joseph sat in silence for a couple of minutes, sipping coffee, thinking their own thoughts. Joseph's mind drifted to the hotel and what the barkeep had said about it. "Plunker, how did the hotel come to burn down? I heard a man speculate today that it might have been set by a local boy."

"No, sir. Whoever said that had to have been talking about Mark Taylor, whose pap runs the mercantile. Mark is simple, but he didn't burn no hotel, no sir."

"How did it catch fire, then?"

"Nobody knows. Maybe just an accident. But I believe somebody set it. Not Mark Taylor, though. Somebody else."

Joseph sensed that Plunker's tongue was starting to loosen, probably mostly because of the liquor he'd put in his coffee. "Who?"

Plunker glanced around as if the walls might suddenly have grown ears. "You know the name of Crane Hart Maxwell, maybe?"

"Of course." Joseph chuckled as he said it; every American knew the name of Crane Hart Maxwell.

"They say he's got more money than God, you know. They say he'll be president of these United States one day, if ever he wants to be."

"What does he have to do with the hotel fire?"

"I believe he set it, sir."

"What?" Joseph chuckled again.

But Plunker remained dead serious. "I said what I

said, sir. I believe that Crane Hart Maxwell is the reason we ain't got no hotel here no more."

That liquor in Plunker's cup must be potent stuff, thought Joseph. "Why would someone like that burn down a hotel?"

"I don't know he done it on purpose. All I can tell you is that the great Mr. Maxwell himself stopped in town, with all kinds of helpers swarming over him like bees around their queen. Then all at once the hotel burns. The fire started somewhere around the big room where Mr. Maxwell was staying. I got a friend worked in that hotel, sweeping floors, and he says it started right in that room. There was a fight, Maxwell squabbling with some young woman. Then there was fire."

"A young woman? Maxwell's a little old for consorting with a young woman . . . and a little married, too."

"I don't think he's a good man, sir. I don't think he is. I think he's quite a sinner."

Joseph nodded, but it was merely in acknowledgment, not agreement. Plunker was talking obvious nonsense. Maxwell had been governor of Massachusetts twice and served two terms in the United States Senate. He was a man birth had blessed with old family money and business success had blessed with new fortunes atop the old. The prevailing notion across the country was that it was only a matter of time before Maxwell moved into the White House. He had been frequently in the newspapers for a year as he made a contrived and highly publicized tour of the nation, ostensibly to collect material for a book he planned to write about the glories of westward expansion and his vision of the nation's destiny. Most believed the tour and the upcoming book were mechanisms to earn Maxwell tremendous public exposure as a prelude to a presidential race. Everything Maxwell did, in fact, seemed designed to attract attention and press coverage. He'd recently married the beautiful widow of a former governor of Ohio; the lavish ceremony had been the subject of lengthy stories and illustrations in almost every newspaper and magazine in America and many in other parts of the world. Maxwell had given the event a populist twist by staging it outdoors and opening an overlooking hillside to the public so that the masses, no matter how lowly, could watch the Great One take his vows with one of the nation's most eligible and lovely widows.

The last Joseph had heard, Maxwell's tour had circled down to Texas, where he had received typically grandiose receptions from the rich and powerful, and admiring applause from the more common folk.

Joseph suddenly felt very tired. It had been a long

day, and he'd covered many miles both by train and horseback. His injured left hand hurt enough that he feared it would keep him awake.

Time to end this conversation and get some sleep. But Joseph's host was in a talkative mood. The longer Plunker drank, though, the less intelligible his talk was, and the more rambling. Joseph quit listening to the words, only to their hypnotic rhythm, and eventually dozed off in his chair.

He awakened in the night to see Plunker's chair empty. He heard the old man snoring off in a tiny side bedroom.

Joseph's blankets had been moved off the floor and spread across his lap and chest. Plunker had tucked him in! Plunker had taken in a stranger and tucked him in like a child.

He moved the blankets back to the floor and lay down again. Within a minute he was again oblivious to the world, sleeping deeply and without dreams.

4

Head bowed, eyes averted away from all he passed, Liam strode down the boardwalk and cut quickly into the hotel and toward the staircase.

"Evening, sir," said the smiling clerk.

"Evening," Liam muttered. He took the stairs two at a time, heading up two flights and turning off the upper landing into the hallway. A woman came down the hall the other way, and he quickly faked a cough so he could lower his head and turn away, hiding his face from her behind the brim of his hat.

He fumbled a key from his vest pocket and opened the door of the last room on the right at the end of the hall. Inside, he lit a lamp and went to the mirror over the dresser, looked at his reflection, and groaned.

The flesh around his eye was already turning blue-black. Jennifer Jacques was quite a pugilist.

"I can't believe she did that," he muttered as he examined the injured, bloodshot orb and the oval bruise that surrounded it. "Can't believe it."

He'd been slapped by many women in his time. This was the first time one had used her fist.

"She must have been raised with brothers," he muttered to his reflection. "Any woman who can hit like that had to have been raised with brothers."

He deserved it, he supposed. But he'd honestly thought she wanted him to kiss her. Wouldn't have tried it if he hadn't been nearly sure of it.

Turning his head this way and that, he examined his still-darkening eye socket and thanked the sky that Joseph wasn't there to see it. He'd be on the floor with laughter.

Liam threw himself down on the bed, put his hands behind his head, and fumed at the ceiling. What trouble women could be! Why in the world the Creator had to make them so unreadable, so inconstant, so troublesome, Liam had no idea. If ever he made it to heaven, he'd ask that question before any other.

Struck in the eye by the fist of a woman! Downright shameful.

"Well," he said aloud, "I'll be hung by the heels before I'll lie around here moping because of some woman. Devil take her! Let her hit *him* in the eye!"

He rose, examined his eye in the mirror one more time, and began mentally composing lies to explain it. He'd come up with something heroic. Hit in the eye by a highwayman trying to rob a parson, or a thief he'd stopped from breaking into an orphanage. Anything but the embarrassing truth.

He closed the door behind him and went looking for a bottle and a good game of cards. He'd had his fill of female company that night.

An hour later, he was a happy man. A strong cigar sat comfortably on his whiskey-dampened lower lip, bright lights and smoke and noise and laughter surrounded him, and the cards were kind. His black eye didn't hurt much, and nobody seemed to care how he'd received it. Life was good.

That train crash had proven to be a fortuitous thing. If not for it, he'd be far away from here, somewhere up the tracks and on the way to Montana with Joseph. He'd have missed out on winning the sixty dollars now piled before him on the table.

Another shuffle, another deal. Liam played his hand stone-faced, unreadable. And won again.

The night grew older and luck did not diminish. By now he was even happy that Jennifer Jacques—annoying woman, now that he thought back on her, and not even all that beautiful—had treated him badly. He had won nearly $150 so far. That was more pleasurable at the moment than the company of any woman.

The key to making money at cards is knowing when to quit, and Liam's instinct didn't fail him. Another couple of successful hands, and he smiled at the sullen group around him. "Gentlemen, it's been a pleasure," he said, gathering his money. "But I'm a growing little boy and need my sleep. My money and I will take our leave just now, and give you our most sincere thanks."

Someone across the table muttered a curse, and the man beside him got up in a huff and headed for the bar, saying something about blacking Liam's other eye. But nobody tried anything. Liam had played honestly and skillfully, and they all knew it. When a man was lucky, he was lucky.

Liam had drunk whiskey tonight, but not to excess, especially when he saw he was destined to win big at the table. There were those in places like this who quietly watched when a man made money and quietly followed him when he left. If any followed him out of there, he would be ready, and sober enough to take care of himself.

He stopped at the bar long enough to buy himself a cheap bottle of whiskey, and a round for the players he'd just cleaned out, just to show that he was a good fellow. Bottle in hand, he exited to the street and headed for his hotel.

He thought at first he was followed, but it proved untrue. Just a businessman going home late from some office down the street. Liam headed for his hotel, much happier than the last time he'd done that. He hoped he didn't run into the pugilistic Miss

Jacques, but if he did, he'd grin at her and wave the whiskey bottle before her face just to annoy her.

He did not encounter Jennifer Jacques, or anyone else he knew. At the end of the hall he stopped and pulled out his key, but as he put it into the lock, the door swung inward at the mere pressure of the key's touch.

Liam stood unmoving, brows lowering as he stared at the open door. Hadn't he locked it when he left? Evidently not . . . thinking back, he couldn't clearly recall having done so. He'd been in a hurry to get out, distracted by his blackened eye and his desire for a card game.

He stepped inside, fired up a lamp, and looked around. All looked as it had before. Everything all right, he decided. He closed and locked the door.

Liam lit a second lamp on the far side of the room, uncorked the whiskey, took a swig right from the bottle, and flopped down on the bed, there to recount the money he'd won. A hundred fifty-eight dollars! He grinned. A rich and content man. He took another celebratory swallow of whiskey, enjoying the burn of it down his throat.

Stacking his bills as neatly as possible on the bedside table and laying his change atop it to hold the bills in place, he leaned back against the headboard and gingerly felt his blackened eye. A little swollen, but not too bad. And it didn't hurt very much. By morning he'd have come up with a cover story to tell Joseph when he got back. In a way, he didn't much care if Joseph got back on time at all. If they missed the train, he'd have another night in town, another chance to play cards where his luck seemed so strong.

He drank a couple of more swigs, then corked the bottle and set it on the bedside table beside the money. Rising, he went to the mirror and looked at his eye, hopeful it had reached the full extent of its bruising. As he leaned forward, looking into the mirror, he froze suddenly. He'd caught a hint of movement in the reflection of the room behind him . . . movement under the bed, beneath the edge of the dingy dust ruffle that hung from the bottom of the mattress to the floor.

Liam had spent nights in more than one rat-infested hotel room, but he'd never made peace with that kind of thing. He turned quickly, headed to the bed, began to kneel, reaching for the dust ruffle.

More movement, but this time at his window. The vaguest hint of a shadow moving across the curtained window, as if someone had walked past. How could that be, though? He was on the third floor.

Then he remembered. He'd forgotten the long, three-decked porch at the front of the hotel, running the width of the building on all three levels and accessible by French windows from some of the more expensive rooms, Liam's not being among those. There was no porch exit from his room except the window itself.

He couldn't recall if the porch was accessible from the street. Maybe someone had followed him from the saloon after all and climbed an outer porch staircase, if there was one. But more likely it was just one of the residents of another room, out strolling on the porch for a nighttime smoke before retiring.

Liam reached down, pulled back the dust ruffle, and almost let out a yell. But the young and clearly terrified woman looking back at him from under the bed stopped him from doing so by placing a finger across her lips, her large, moist eyes moving, flicking in the direction of the door.

Momentarily paralyzed by surprise, it took Liam a moment to react and look in the indicated direction. He saw a vague shadow moving in the space between the bottom of the door and the floor. Someone was in the hall, lingering at his door.

Liam looked back at the young woman's face—quite a pretty face, he couldn't help but notice—and received from its intense and fearful look a message: Whoever was at the door was there because of her, and she desperately did not want to be found.

"I'll go see," Liam whispered to her.

"No!" she whispered back urgently. But he'd already let the dust ruffle fall, hiding her.

He didn't know what was going on here, who she was or who was at the door or why they were after her, but he wasn't one to endure strangers lurking in

47

ominous silence outside his room. Liam opened the wardrobe, pulled his pistol from the holster that he'd hung inside it earlier, and crept to the door.

He stuck the pistol under his left arm as he quickly turned the key. He yanked the door wide open and faced the man just beyond it, getting his pistol back in hand at the same time. He faced a big fellow, middle-aged, with sandy hair, wide mustache, weathered face. Evil eyes. Cold and dark. They widened a moment in surprise at being confronted, then narrowed again. The man did not step back.

"Who are you and what do you want?" Liam said, pistol in hand and deliberately not hidden. He noticed that the man was armed, too, a gun belt around his waist despite the fact he was in a town where a sign right out on the main street proclaimed that the local gun law forbade the wearing of arms inside the town limits.

"My name's Murphy," the man said. "I'm looking for my daughter."

"You may notice that I ain't her, and I'm alone here. Move on, Murphy. I don't like folks I don't know hanging around my door like a shadow."

Murphy's eyes flicked to the right, looking past Liam, then back to Liam's face again. He smiled ever so slightly. "Beg pardon, sir. Evening." He turned and walked down the hall, Liam watching him go.

5

Liam closed the door, locked it, then turned and saw something he'd not noticed before. A lace handkerchief on the floor, trimmed in red and yellow. A woman's item, obviously dropped in haste, lying right in the area that Murphy had looked at when his gaze had flicked into the room.

So now Murphy, if that was really his name, knew Liam was lying. He knew the young woman was here.

Liam picked up the handkerchief and went back to the bed. Lifting the dust ruffle, he glared at her and handed her the handkerchief.

"Yours, I presume, Miss Murphy?"

"Please . . . don't let them find me! My name isn't Murphy, and that wasn't my father."

"There's more than one after you? Why? And who?"

"Please, don't let them know I'm here!"

"I think they do know. The one in the hall does, anyway. I think he saw this handkerchief. Why did you come to this room?"

"You have to protect me! Please!"

"How about you come out from under this bed? It's a little hard to talk like this."

"You'll protect me?"

"Maybe. But I want some answers. I want to know why the devil you've come into my room. And I want to know why that man is after you."

She came out from under the bed and stood, trembling. But Liam could tell it wasn't fear of him as a stranger that made her shiver. Whoever was after her had her terrified. She stared at the door.

"Is it locked?" she asked.

"It is now. It wasn't when I came in."

"Thank God it wasn't locked. I couldn't have gotten in . . . I would have been trapped by them in the hall."

"Did you take the luck of the draw or pick my room in particular to come to?"

"I picked it."

"Why?"

"Because of your name. I was running, trying to find a place to escape them. The register was open on the desk downstairs and I saw your name and the number of your room. I thought maybe you would help me. Because of your name . . . I even hoped you might by some miracle prove to be . . . never mind."

"What do you mean, because of my name? And just who are you?"

"I am April McCree. You would not know me."

Liam looked her over and thought that she looked like just the kind he would like to know. Long hair, auburn, quite thick and with long and seemingly natural curls. Face pale, unblemished, eyes brown and deep as canyon pools. April McCree was beauty incarnate . . . beauty at the moment overtaken by terror. The fear in her expression was palpable.

"Who is after you, and why?"

"It's because of Pat, you see. They're after me because Pat and I betrayed—"

A click at the window, ever so faint, metal brushing glass . . .

Liam remembered the man on the porch. At the window now. That noise—a pistol barrel, grazing the window?

"Oh, God preserve me, and God preserve my poor, unborn child!" April said in a sharp and very Irish-inflected whisper, and dropped to the floor, huddling beside the bed.

Swearing beneath his breath, Liam hurried to the window and threw open the curtain. A young man, thin and raggedly whiskered, leaped back with eyes wide, and dropped the pistol in his hand. Liam tugged at the window to open it. Stuck! He pulled harder and the window went up, then jammed. He yanked at it some more.

The young man on the porch scrambled for his dropped pistol, but so hurriedly that he fumbled about, unable to pick it up. At last he got it, by the barrel, but instead of trying to use it just ran off down the porch and to the staircase at the end of it. Liam got the window open and made it out and onto the porch, but the scared rabbit had already descended nearly to the street.

Pistol in hand, Liam went after him, bounding down the stairs. He saw the fellow's long legs flailing as he rounded the corner of a building and vanished into an alley. Liam pursued, but at the end of the alley was struck by a bolt of common sense and decided not to enter. The man could be poised back in the alley, pistol out and ready to fire at Liam as soon as he let himself be outlined against the lesser darkness of the street.

Liam swore again and gave up the chase. Whoever the scared man was, he'd escaped.

He remembered Murphy then. Probably still inside the hotel . . . and that door, though now locked, could be kicked in. Liam raced back to the base of the porch staircase and up to the third level and his open window.

He reentered his room, gasping for breath, and

felt his heart leap to his throat when he saw the door was open. He went to it, examined it, found it had not been kicked in, but opened from the inside. He quickly searched the room, looking under the bed, in the wardrobe. She was gone. Fled the room while he chased the scared rabbit from the porch.

Liam looked up and down every hallway, descended to the lobby and searched there, then outside and all around the hotel. She was not to be found.

He returned to his room, hoping she had returned there while he was out looking for her. She had not. He closed the door, then went to the window and closed it as well, drawing the curtains across it.

Blowing out the lamps, he sat in darkness, wondering who she was and why she had come to him . . . and who *they* were and why they pursued her.

Unborn child. She'd said those words. *God preserve my poor, unborn child.*

So she was pregnant. Alone, pursued, pregnant, and very scared.

Liam sat in the darkness for an hour, hoping she would come back. When she did not, he left the hotel and wandered the street until long after midnight, trying to find her. But the luck that had befriended him at the poker table earlier was no longer with him. He found no trace of her.

The poker table . . .

He returned quickly to the hotel and entered his room. The money was gone from the bedside table. He'd not even noticed.

He did not feel anger, oddly, though the evidence was clear that she'd robbed him. He felt instead disappointed. He had always trusted his impressions, and his impression of her was not of a charlatan or thief. The terror on her face surely had been no mere act.

But he forced himself to consider whether the entire thing—the hiding, the pretense of being pursued, the men at the door and window—might have been a conspiratorial charade, the girl working along with the supposed gunmen.

No. If all that activity had been nothing more than a mechanism to get the money on his bedside table, that could have been achieved simply by walking in and taking it.

Pat. She'd said the name Pat. And she'd said she'd been drawn to this room because of the name on the register. Carrigan.

Pat Carrigan.

Locking his room, laying his pistol on the bedside table within easy reach, he lay down fully clothed and stared into the darkness until he fell asleep.

6

Breakfast was fried pork and biscuits baked heavy on the lard and topped with some of the richest and saltiest gravy that Joseph had ever encountered. He was stuffed before he'd downed half a plateful, but kept going because Plunker had gone to a lot of effort to cook it all, and was going at his own sizable portion like a man who took eating very seriously. Joseph wondered how he managed to stay so thin.

"You're going off today, I reckon," Plunker said.

"I am. I have to leave soon to catch a train over in Culpepperville."

Plunker nodded and took another bite of biscuit, looking at Joseph with eyes that reminded Joseph of a sad old hound he'd raised when he'd been a boy, only to see it die for unidentifiable reasons before it was three years old.

"Reckon you'll ever be coming back through here?"

"Well, not that I know of, Plunker, but a man never knows."

"If you do, I hope you'll stop by. Say hello."

"I'll do it." Joseph forced his stuffed stomach to accommodate one more bite of pork. "Maybe we can have coffee again. You make a cup of coffee a man can sink his teeth into."

"Wish I'd get more company. A man likes company."

"I'll come back and see you. I'll do it."

Plunker smiled and forked another slice of pork onto his plate.

"Where'd you get all this pork?" Joseph asked.

"Mr. Taylor. The same one we talked about, the father of the simple boy. He's kind to me."

Joseph left Plunker's place with a degree of honest regret. He was an easy man to like. And clearly a lonely one in his old age and racial isolation in a dismal, anonymous little town.

Something drew Joseph back to the empty lot where he'd seen the rubbish being burned. He dismounted and poked around the cold ash heap, kicking at the remnants of this and that, and thinking about the young Pat Carrigan who had been taken to an unknown fate out on the plains. The same last name as Joseph's own, and the same first name as his missing uncle. A connection? A coincidence? He'd probably never know.

"Hey, hey."

Joseph turned. A round-faced boy, freckled, older

at second glance than he appeared at first, approached him, grinning. "Hey, hey."

"Hello," Joseph said. "I'll bet your name is Mark."

"How'd you know?"

"Somebody told me about you. I took a guess."

"Who you? Why you looking at my burning place?"

"My name's Carrigan. Joseph Carrigan."

Mark Taylor stopped, brows knitting. "Carrigan."

"That's right. There was a sign you burned, right here, that had that name on it. I saw it when the train went by yesterday."

"That was the fist man's sign."

"The fist man . . . like this?" Joseph feigned a couple of punches.

Mark Taylor did the same, vigorously. "Yeah, yeah. The fist man. He was good with fists. Fast, like shooting bullets. Real fast. Swoosh, swoosh!"

"I hear he isn't here anymore."

"He's dead now. Everybody says he's dead. Somebody took him away, and now he's dead."

"Did you know him?"

"I seen him." He swished his fists through the air again. "He could fight good. I wish I could fight good."

"Best thing is to avoid fights if you can."

"You got his same name. Carrigan."

"Yes."

"You his brother? Because you look kind of like him."

"No."

"His father?"

"No. I'm not old enough for that."

"No. You ain't. Because his father's name is Patrick."

"He told you that?"

"Yeah. I'm like that, too. I got two names. My first name is Mark, but my middle name is Jim. Like my father."

"How do I look like him?"

"Your eyes. You look the same in the eyes."

"Did Pat Carrigan tell you where his father lives?"

"No."

"You sure about the names being the same, father and son?"

"Yeah."

Joseph kicked at a chunk of charred wood. "Well, better be going. Good to meet you, young man."

"Good to meet you, too, sir."

A haze of woodsmoke overhung the town of Culpepperville when Joseph rode in. He paused in front of a store just opening for the day. A man in a dirty white apron was sweeping off the porch.

"Morning . . . could you tell me, sir, which hotel the folks from the train derailment were put up in last night?"

"Turn right at that corner. Three buildings down. Big long porches on all levels. You can't miss it."

Joseph didn't miss it. He dismounted in front of

the hotel. While tying his horse to the rail, something fell beside his foot. It was the smoldering butt of a cigar, well chewed. Joseph looked up and saw Liam leaning over the rail, looking down at him.

"See you made it safe and sound, brother."

"I did."

"Had breakfast?"

"I have. But I could eat some more."

"I got a couple of biscuits with ham up here. Leftover. You're welcome to it."

Joseph climbed the outer staircase and joined Liam on the porch. Liam had taken his chair again and sat leaned back, his feet propped up on the rail.

"Any luck with finding that sign?"

"A little. There really was a sign. And there really is a Pat Carrigan . . . not our uncle, though. This is a young fellow. But I'm wondering if he might be a cousin."

"Whoa. Back up and tell me more."

"Biscuits first. Where's the door to your room?"

"Right there. It slides up and down and has curtains just behind it."

"Nicely designed hotel."

Joseph entered via the window and emerged with his biscuits and ham. Pulling up a chair, he sat down beside Liam, ate a few bites, then told the story of his visit to the town of Hooper and the things he'd learned there.

"What do you think, Liam? The boy told me that Pat Carrigan had the same name as his father. It could be him, you know. We don't know much about our uncle. He could have an army of children for all we know. That could be our own cousin who was taken out onto the plains and killed."

"Maybe. If that really happened. You don't really know . . . it's all just rumors at a railroad stop."

"Maybe. But it makes me all the more determined to find our uncle. I'm more eager than ever to get on to Montana."

"Good. Enjoy the trip. I ain't going."

"What?"

"I'm staying here. For a while, anyway."

"Why the devil do you want to do that?"

"I had an interesting evening."

"Go on."

Liam took a deep breath and told his tale. Joseph listened, wordless, and held his silence a few moments even after Liam was through.

"Liam, are you serious about this? You want to stay here to find some saloon girl who stole your gambling earnings?"

"I do."

"That strikes me as foolish."

"I'm surprised to hear you say that. You've always been one to protect the downtrodden, particularly when they wear dresses."

60

"Liam, I don't know why anyone would have gone to so much trouble just to steal a cache of poker money, but the entire thing surely was a deception of some sort. Most likely this poor young woman you're so caught up with has already divided up the money with her partners and is hiding under somebody else's bed, ready to tell her woeful tale and shed some more tears."

"If she'd just been after the money, she could have just taken it off the bedside table and been gone. I'd have never even seen her."

"Maybe they figured on something more than that, but realized you were a chicken with too few feathers to be worth the plucking."

"Or maybe she was telling the truth. I'm telling you, Joseph, she was frightened. Not acting, not trying to get my money or steal my watch or seduce me or anything of that sort. She was scared, pure scared, and those men who were looking for her really were after her."

Joseph put his own feet up on the rail, and glanced at his pocket watch, put the watch back into his vest, and pulled his coat around him a little tighter against a cool morning wind. "All right. So she's a woman truly in trouble, and somebody is truly after her. Why does that make her our business? There are a lot of people out there with worries and woes and enemies, and we can't take on every problem we run across."

"Nobody said anything about 'we.' You want to go on to Montana, go ahead. I can always find you later."

"I don't want to split up, Liam. We should do whatever we do together."

"There's something about her I didn't mention, Joseph. Two things, actually. The first is she's going to have a baby."

Joseph frowned. "How do you know?"

"Something she said. 'God preserve me, and my poor unborn child.' She said it when she thought they were going to get to her. She was truly afraid, and not just for herself, but for her baby. She's pregnant, alone, and there are some vicious men after her. I want to know why, and I want to help her if I can."

"Unborn child."

"That's right."

Joseph stared at his boots. "Well . . . that does give a man pause. How can you know she was telling the truth?"

"I can't. But I believe she was."

"What was the second thing you didn't tell me?"

"She mentioned the name Pat Carrigan. She came into my room because she saw the Carrigan name on the register, and she hoped that I might be Pat. Then everything fell apart, and there was no time for her to tell me more."

Down on the street, others who had been on the train with the Carrigan brothers began to appear, bearing luggage and heading toward the train station. A distant wail gave tidings of an approaching locomotive.

"There's your train," Liam said. "If you want to catch it, you'd best move."

Joseph took a long, slow breath. "I don't reckon that will be the last train to head up that track. And I doubt Montana is going to go anywhere."

"You're staying?"

"Reckon so."

"That's good."

"More likely it's foolish. But it isn't the first time I've been a fool."

"That's for sure the truth. I could write a book about all the times you've been a fool."

"How are we going to find this April McCree?"

"It's a small town. We just look. And ask a few questions."

"Starting when?"

"Now's as good a time as any."

"And what about the men after her? Can you give me a description?"

Liam did, as best he could. "The one at the window was cowardly," he concluded. "He ran like a rabbit just at the sight of me. The one in the hall was colder, bigger, stronger. Older, too. He had eyes a rattlesnake would envy. Watch out for him."

"I will."

7

An hour later, Joseph stood at the edge of town, watching the train upon which he had expected to ride vanishing toward the horizon. He chuckled to himself, reflecting upon the odd turns of life. What had begun as a simple railroad journey toward Montana had been thrown off course not only once, but twice, once by a derailment, and now by the intervention in Liam's life of a young woman who, despite Liam's conviction, could turn out to be no more than a confidence artist.

But what did it matter? Liam was clearly convinced that searching for her was worth doing, and the truth was, they could afford the time. Their most recent independent business venture, a cattle drive, had failed miserably. Their effort to find their uncle, though heartfelt, was itself something they had seized upon only when all other options seemed to dissolve. If they put it off for a day or two, what could it hurt?

Joseph turned and saw Liam approaching, buttoning the fly of his trousers after having paused behind a woodshed to relieve himself. Liam eyed the departing train.

"Ah, well, I guess we really are left behind now."

"We'll catch another one later. Meanwhile, I suppose we should get started looking."

"Yep. I've been thinking, Joseph: let's split up and just walk the town a bit. We could cover it quicker that way."

"It would be a more interesting task done with company."

"That's true, but you've also got to consider that she knows my face. If she sees me out searching, she'll probably hide, figuring I'm after her trying to get my money back. So you may have an advantage searching alone. She won't know you."

"Good point. We'll do it your way. But I'll have a disadvantage. There could be other women who look like April McCree."

"You'll know April McCree if you see her. The most beautiful auburn hair I've ever seen, except maybe that of the girl who grew up two doors down from us in Nashville. Remember her? But April has a prettier face. Her skin is fair, and her eyes are big and so sad they'll break your heart. But, oh, she's beautiful! If your heart starts racing and your blood gets hot in your veins, you've seen her."

"That fine a creature, is she?"

"She is."

"Let's meet again at, say, one o'clock, over there at that cafe on the end of the street. We can have some lunch and then keep searching if we haven't found her yet. Joseph, I've been thinking. What if the ones who took Pat Carrigan out on the plains and killed him are the same ones now after April McCree?"

Joseph scratched at his chin, an unconscious gesture he sometimes made when afflicted by troubling thoughts. He used his injured hand, but winced and changed to the other. "We really do need to find her."

"Then let's get started."

The town was split almost exactly down the middle by Main Street, so the brothers divided their search areas accordingly. They searched Main Street together, poking in stores, eyeing windows and alleys, even glancing into smokehouses and woodsheds and outbuildings. They did not find April McCree nor anyone who seemed aware of her; nor did they spot any men who resembled those who pursued her. Once Main Street was searched, they divided, Liam taking the northern half of town, Joseph the southern.

The day was clear but brisk, the kind that gave Liam vigor and a clear mind. They'd left their horses at the hotel stables, figuring this job was one easier done on foot. The exercise was good. Train rides and such had of late rendered him less active than he liked to be, so he took to this activity with enthusiasm.

He had a feeling in his gut that he'd find her. An intuitive feeling, the validity of which only time would reveal. He tried to think like a young woman on the run. Where would he hide? Not the hotel. Too visible, and she'd robbed Liam there and wouldn't be prone to stay in such proximity to him.

There was another possibility. She might have taken that stolen money and bought a ticket on that same train that had just pulled out. If so, then their search was not only futile but ironic: By staying behind to find her, they'd lost her.

But Liam didn't believe she was on the train. The men after her probably watched the train station. The kind of running she was doing wouldn't likely be done on a public conveyance.

Culpepperville was a somewhat more substantial town than Liam had realized. What at first glance seemed a relatively small cluster of houses and businesses revealed itself on closer inspection to be comprised of several inhabited blocks. Here on the northern side of town, seemingly the poorer side, houses were small and numerous, and it was difficult to do much investigating without looking suspicious.

Liam wondered if he might stumble across the same men who'd been at the hotel. If so, he'd have some talking to do with them, and maybe more. Gun law or not, his pistol was secured under his long-tailed coat, belted up high so it wouldn't show. He'd insisted that Joseph wear his as well.

A woman in a bonnet and shawl passed, carrying a basket of freshly baked bread toward a rickety little stand on the corner of the street. She reminded Liam of some of the old Irishwomen he'd known growing up back on a predominately Irish block in Nashville, where he and Joseph had scrapped their way up in a hardscrabble world that offered few niceties to Irishmen. They'd done it without the benefit of a mother, but their father, God rest him, had done well by his sons. Never a man of monetary means, he had been rich instead in loyalty, courage, and perseverance, and these he'd passed on to his boys. To Liam he'd also passed along a fondness for cards, whiskey, and gambling—vices that gave Liam more trouble than anything else, but which he loved even so.

By golly, he'd have a loaf of that bread, which smelled so like home and childhood and the kitchens of neighbors forever gone. Even the old Nashville neighborhood itself was gone, flattened to make room for some rich man's mansion. Liam had been depressed for three days when he heard the news.

"Good morning to you, ma'am," Liam said. The old woman looked up and peered at him from beneath the curving brim of her bonnet, like a squirrel peering out of a hole in a tree, her thin lips curling tightly into the smallest of smiles.

"Good morning, sir." She eyed Liam up and down, quickly, and he was amused at this subtle affirmation that age did not necessarily diminish a woman's eye for a fine-looking man.

"I'm hoping you intend to sell that bread, for I'd like to buy a loaf," he said.

Her eyes twinkled. "Indeed, sir. I baked this very one here for you." She paused and looked at his face. "You've hurt yourself, sir. Your eye is black." Her accent revealed her as Irish.

"Yes, yes, it is. I fought a fellow for a loaf of bread that didn't have half the wonderful aroma of what you've got in that basket."

"I bake it with a touch of beer mixed in, sir. It makes all the difference."

Liam dug for his money. "I don't know if I've smelled a finer aroma of fresh bread since I was a boy, growing up beside Mrs. O'Grady, who baked every day. But she didn't put beer in her dough. Mr. O'Grady kept the beer drunk up." Liam spoke now with a light Irish brogue, something that could come out when he allowed it, which he usually didn't. *Speak like an Irishman and you'll get treated like an Irishman,* his father had always preached. *Learn to sound like a born American, and you'll find your path cleared of many obstacles.* So both Liam and Joseph had grown up resisting the natural inclination to speak as their father spoke, and forced themselves to pick up an American style of speech.

He accepted his paper-wrapped loaf, tore open the paper, and pulled off a hunk of still-steaming bread. He took a bite and closed his eyes in true pleasure. "The touch of a master hand, ma'am, the touch of a master hand. I salute you."

She beamed.

"And now, ma'am, a question: Are you by chance acquainted with one April McCree? A young woman, auburn hair, big brown eyes nearly as lovely as your own."

"I know no such name, sir. But the description sounds like that of my own daughter . . . who surely you'd be pleased to meet."

"Does she bake as well as you?"

"Almost, young man."

"Then I may be in love. But another question: Have you seen any strangers about, either a young woman as I described, or perhaps two men, one of them a big fellow, middle-aged, hair the color of sand, a mustache, face like leather? The other smaller, thin, dark hair—weaselly looking man, with a beard that looks like dirt on his face?"

"That would be my husband." She said it so seriously that it took Liam a moment to notice the teasing in her eyes, and laugh. "But in truth, sir, no, I have not seen such men."

"I thank you for your time in any case . . . and for this excellent bread."

"You come around again, sir, and I'll let you meet my daughter."

Liam smiled and nodded, but he'd be making no return visits. Experience had taught him that daughters usually became their mothers—and this woman was a bit too much woman for Liam Carrigan. He doubted he could fully wrap his arms around her if he had to.

"Good day to you, ma'am."

"And a good day to you, sir."

Liam wandered off, nibbling at the bread.

8

Around a corner, then another, nibbling all the while. Then Liam stopped abruptly and stepped behind a scraggly tree.

There he was, the weaselly gunman, the cowardly one whom Liam had chased off the hotel porch. Walking across a back lot barefooted, scratching at the back of his neck, yawning, hair sticking up in all directions like thatch on a badly done Irish roof. The very sight of him brought back to Liam the vision of April McCree's pale face with its beautiful big eyes, her fearful expression, her terror-inspired prayer for herself and her unborn child. Liam glared at the unwitting fellow, who was stumbling sleepily toward a backyard privy, and tossed his loaf of bread to the ground.

The weasel entered the privy, already fumbling with his trousers, and closed the door.

Liam advanced and stood before the privy, waiting. He heard the splatter of liquid into the pit below the outhouse.

He gave the man inside just long enough to re-hitch his fly, then yanked open the privy door, grabbed him by the shoulders, and pulled him down.

The man let out a yelp of terror. Liam was on him in a moment, pinning him, glaring down into his face.

"All right, you scoundrel, talk to me! Tell me who she is and why you are after her!"

The man's lips moved, but no words emerged, only very vague, pitiful noises like an injured animal might make moments before death.

"Speak up!"

"What . . . who . . ."

Liam shook the man, hard. "Talk! Tell me why you were outside my hotel room window with a pistol drawn! Tell me why you and Murphy or whoever he really is are chasing a young woman who's so scared she can hardly get by! Talk!"

"I don't know what you're talking about!"

Liam drew back a fist. The man howled and cringed.

"Talk!"

"I ain't never been at no hotel window! I swear!" And just then, a cold realization came over Liam. This man was telling him the truth. This was not the same face he'd seen at the hotel window. Similar, yes, but not the same man.

Liam froze, fist still up, and realized what a terrible mistake he'd just made.

"Get off him!"

The voice exploded from somewhere behind him. Liam's heart skipped about three beats, and he twisted around reflexively to see who called to him. His nose was assaulted by the combined smells of body odor and whiskey. Then something smashed across the top of his skull and he was washed over with cool liquid and showered with fragments of glass. The whiskey smell grew stronger all at once, and he realized that a whiskey bottle had just been smashed across his head.

Fortunately, it didn't hurt much. The bottle had struck the hardest part of his skull. But the surprise and impact threw him off-kilter, and he lost balance and tilted to one side. The terrified man pinned beneath him shoved upward, and Liam tilted over completely.

The man scrambled to his feet. "Get away from him, Charlie! He's a madman, I tell you! He's a lunatic!"

Liam tried to get up, but the spilled whiskey had puddled beneath him, and he slipped in it and went down on his side. "I'm sorry!" he said. "I've made a mistake!"

"Reckon you have!" said Charlie, who was clad only in filthy long underwear with holes in unfortunate places. He pulled a big, bare, dirt-crusted foot back and kicked Liam in the crotch.

Liam went down, feeling as if the breath had been driven out of him in an explosion that passed through the top of his head. His entire midsection clamped down in the vilest of pain, his throat constricted, and his stomach threatened to heave itself empty. Liam lay on the ground, hurting too badly to move.

Charlie loomed above him, looking down with alternating expressions of triumph and concern. At length triumph won out, and he kicked Liam again, but this time in the thigh, and not quite as hard. "Reckon I showed you, feller," he said. "Don't you go pulling my son out of no outhouse again, hear me? Why'd you do that to a man, anyhow? You some kind of sodomite or something? That what you are?"

"It . . . was . . . just a . . . mistake," Liam managed to gasp out.

"Oh, that it was. I doubt you'll make it again."

"You can . . . count on . . . that . . ."

Liam's victim ventured closer, leaned over, and looked at the suffering man. "No fooling . . . why'd you do it, mister?"

"Thought you . . . were somebody else . . ."

"I think you nigh killed him, Pap."

"Good Lord—there comes the deputy marshal!" Charlie said. "Somebody must have hollered for him. Listen, I got to get inside. They been wanting to find me to ask me about that stolen goat, and I ain't in no humor to talk. You tell them you done this, Joe."

"What?"

"You tell them he attacked you, and you kicked him in the testicockles."

"The what?"

"The testicockles. That's the Christian name for the balls."

Liam groaned. Eye blackened by a woman, "testicockles" flattened by a drunken imbecile. What was next? Being flayed alive by a Sunday school superintendent?

Charlie disappeared. Liam managed to push up to a seated posture. He was eager for privacy and the chance to examine the damage, which he hoped would not have lasting effects.

"Who's this, Joe?" asked the man with the badge when he reached the scene.

"Don't know him. He attacked me. Drug me right out of the privy. I kicked him in the, the . . . test . . . test . . ."

"I know what you mean. You, mister, what's your name?"

"Carrigan . . . Liam Carrigan . . . I thought that he was somebody else."

"But you did attack him?"

"Yes, but I thought—"

"Don't much matter what you thought, does it? You attacked a man right on his own property, or his pap's property, anyway." The lawman leaned over and sniffed. "Phew! Smell that whiskey on you! Early in the day to be so drunk, ain't it, friend?"

"I'm not drunk."

"Yeah, and you ain't no brawler, either. Not with that black eye. Come on, friend, get to your feet. Let's get you to the jail and let you rest this off, and think about the lack of wisdom in attacking folks on their own property when you're drunk as a skunk."

Liam managed to get up, though with pain, but he could hardly stand straight. His walking was a staggering shuffle, and it certainly made him appear drunk. But getting arrested was not as dismaying as it might have been. The jail would have bunks, and just then Liam wanted only to lie down and wait until the throbbing pain went away.

"Best turn away from drink," the deputy counseled Liam, as they headed jailward. "Look what it's doing to you, friend! You can hardly stand up!"

"I got kicked in the crotch."

That seemed to go right past the deputy. "I had a great-uncle who drank himself to death. Got drunk, vomited lying on his back, and drowned in it. Don't let something like that happen to you, friend. The demon drink ain't worth death, nor your soul."

"Death sounds pretty good right at the moment. As for my soul, I think it's been kicked out of me."

"You are drunk indeed, friend. Drunk indeed."

The jail looked just as wretched as a small-town jail can look. A simple clapboard structure, it looked flimsy from the outside, like a man could just walk through the walls if he wanted. The deputy must have read Liam's thoughts, because he said, "Don't let the looks fool you. Ain't nobody ever busted out of either cell we got in there. Stout as a fat old maid, that jail is."

Another man with a badge came out of the front door as Liam, wincing, was helped up onto the porch. This fellow was older and wider and had long gray hair. His badge was bigger, and it was immediately evident this was the head lawman in the town of Culpepperville, and proud of it.

"Who's this?" he asked.

"Name is Carrigan. A drunk who tried to drag Joe Plunkett right out of his privy, God only knows why. Joe defended himself, and one of the neighbors hollered me over. I saw what had gone on, and . . . Lordy! What's this?"

The deputy had just bumped against Liam's hidden pistol. He reached under Liam's coat and pulled it out. "I'll be! Look at this, Marshal! We got a gun law violator here!"

The marshal frowned. "You mean to tell me you didn't search him?"

"Well . . . I . . . uh, no, I didn't do that. I guess I didn't think that . . . well, I should have."

"He could have shot you at any point!"

"I don't shoot lawmen," Liam said.

The marshal put a hand under Liam's chin, lifting his head to get a good look at him. Liam's humility reached its limit. He pulled his head away and shot a murderous look at the lawman. "You lock me up if you want, old man, falsely accuse me, take my pistol, you label me a drunk when I'm sober . . . do all that if you want, but I'll be damned if you're going to paw around on my face like I'm a child and you're my dear old granny."

The marshal cocked up one eyebrow and grinned out of the corner of his mouth. "Got a live one here, I see. All full of spit and vinegar. Funny how a man can drink whiskey and once it's inside him it all turns to spit and vinegar. Funny thing."

"I'll lock him up," the deputy said.

"Got to make room if you do. I got both cells full."

"Oh . . . I didn't know that."

"There's a lot you don't seem to know. Like whether your prisoners are carrying arms while being under arrest."

"I'm sorry. I should have done better, Marshal."

"Don't let it happen again. But listen: One of

the prisoners in there is naught but a fellow I locked up for poking around some houses and scaring a few women, and bearing a pistol inside town limits. He's been in long enough. I'll turn him out and old spit and vinegar here can take his place."

The marshal turned and entered the jail, leaving Liam alone with the deputy, who put his hand on Liam's shoulder as if to hold him in place. Liam jerked free. "Get your hand off me! I'll not run off . . . and believe me, if I wanted to, you'd not be able to stop me."

"I'd have to shoot you, and I would. You made me look like a fool in front of the marshal, hiding that pistol."

"You made yourself look like a fool for not thinking to look for it. I was wondering when you'd get around to it."

Liam moved in such a way that a new throb of pain rippled through him. He bowed his head and squeezed his eyes closed. At this point the door opened; he heard the marshal's voice, felt him and the newly freed prisoner brush past him.

Liam opened his eyes and caught a passing glimpse of the man just released. Liam stiffened, his pain suddenly forgotten, his attention at once focused on the man who passed him.

It was the cold-eyed man he'd confronted at the

door of his hotel room, the one who had called himself Murphy.

"You! You there! I want to talk to you!" Liam bellowed.

Liam dodged around the deputy, lunging toward the cold-eyed man, who wheeled and turned a glaring gaze upon him.

The deputy was upon Liam at once, pulling him back; the marshal reached for his pistol.

"That man there, he's been hunting a young woman, threatening her!" Liam shouted. "I've been looking for that man!"

Murphy looked at the marshal. "I don't know what he's talking about. I've never seen that man before."

"That's a lie! Arrest that man, Marshal! Arrest him!"

"You're plumb loco, friend," the deputy said, pulling Liam toward the jail. "Where the hell did you come from? Get in that jail!"

Deputy and marshal together hustled Liam through the door. He twisted, looking over his shoulder at Murphy, who held his gaze for the long moment it took for Liam to be forced indoors. Then he turned and was gone.

9

At one time, the house had been quite fine, nearly a mansion. Approached from the north, it looked substantially intact. But a slight change of angle revealed the truth: The house was a shell, heavily damaged on three sides by a windstorm or perhaps a tornado. No one lived there any longer . . . no one could.

But if so, why had Joseph just caught a glimpse of a woman moving past a window on what remained of the second floor?

He walked to the front door, which stood slightly ajar because the frame of the door was twisted out of shape, and looked inside. "Hello?"

No reply. Joseph hesitated, pushed open the door a few inches making a loud creak, and entered. Empty. A couple of ruined chairs, a broken-down table, a massive sideboard with the doors barely hanging on, home now to mice and rats. The storm that had done the house in had made a good job of it.

Inside the house's shadowed interior, he had a strong feeling of being alone. But he was certain that he had seen a woman in the window, and brief as the glimpse was, it had given him an impression of auburn hair, pale skin . . . and who else but a woman on the run would enter such a damaged and dangerous building? If the woman he'd seen was anyone but April McCree, he would be quite surprised.

Joseph took a few steps forward and almost fell when a floorboard rocked beneath his weight. He managed to dance off onto firmer footing without losing his balance. He drew in his breath sharply and let it out slowly, glad he hadn't fallen and been forced to catch himself on his damaged fingers.

Veering around the more obviously unstable parts of the floor, Joseph headed for the staircase. It creaked loudly underfoot as he climbed, and in the middle section were three stairs that were missing entirely. Looking down into the hole, he saw the floor of the closet under the staircase. It was splintered and broken, obviously wrenched to pieces when the house was wind damaged. Joseph carefully stepped over the missing stairs and pulled himself up on the rail.

To his right on the second floor was a wall that

extended all the way to the ceiling alongside the staircase, hiding any view of the upper hall beyond it. Anticipating that she was hiding in that hall or one of the rooms that opened onto it, Joseph paused at the top stair and decided to make his presence and good intentions known before showing himself, just in case she was armed.

"Ma'am, I know you're up here, and I want to assure you that I will do you no harm. In fact, my intention is to help you if I can, if you are the person I believe you are. Is your name—"

He had no time to finish the question. From around the other side of the wall that blocked his view, a figure appeared and shoved hard against him, knocking him down. He hit the stairs hard, tumbled, rolled until he reached those missing stairs. He plunged down into the closet below, onto the ruined floor, then through that to the dark and very deep cellar, where he landed with a hard thump that drove the breath out of him and sent stars spiraling across the black field of his vision.

The cell was nothing but a box made of heavy, flat, iron bars. Even the ceiling was comprised of crossed bars of iron. Liam lay on a hard bunk that must have been rescued from a medieval torture chamber and stared at the bars above him, thinking how convenient they would be for any prisoner inclined to hang himself. This was truly an accommodating jail.

"What'd you do?" asked the prisoner in the other iron box across from Liam's.

Liam mumbled, "I killed a man. Tore his head clean off and roasted it on a stick. I'd only got to eat half of it when they got me, blast 'em."

"Same thing happened to me. Well, no . . . truth is I just got a little drunk and rowdy yesterday, and tried to knock the noggin off my wife's meddlesome sister. From the way you were staggering and smelling just now, I figure maybe you've been on the bottle some, too."

"I was walking that way because I got kicked in the testicockles, as someone put it."

"The what?"

"Never mind. And the reason I smell like whiskey is that somebody busted a bottle of it across my head."

"That's a waste of good whiskey."

"Amen. I could use a few good swallows of it right now."

"I hit the bottle a little too much. My sister-in-law keeps trying to get me on the path of the straight and narrow, and that just makes me get drunk even more. So I spend a good bit of time in this jail. The bunk over here is better than the one you got over there. Next time you should try to get this cell. My name's Henry Barger, by the way."

"Liam Carrigan. Good to know you."

"Irish name. You don't sound Irish."

"I was raised in Nashville, native-born American." The latter half was a lie, but Liam had found it easier to get on in the United States if people perceived him as a natural citizen.

The door to the cellblock opened, and someone entered. Liam lifted his head, hopeful that by some unexpected circumstance Joseph had learned where he was and had come to spring him. But the person entering was just a boy, maybe thirteen or fourteen, and he headed straight for the cell of Liam's neighbor.

"Pap! Do you know who you been in here with?" he asked, excited. "Do you know?"

"What are you talking about, son?"

"The man who was in here before and they just let loose. I saw him leaving. You know who it was?"

"He told me his name is Jack something."

"Murphy?" Liam contributed. The boy wheeled and looked at him when he spoke, said nothing, turned to his father again.

"Yeah, Murphy. He said he was Jack Murphy."

"No, no. I've seen way too many pictures. That was Hank Coldwell. *The* Hank Coldwell!"

Liam smiled subtly, and Henry Barger laughed

out loud. "That's right, son, and the fellow in the cell now is Jesse James."

"I ain't lying, Pap! I've seen two different camera-took pictures of Hank Coldwell, and that's him! I swear it!"

"Why do you think they'd have let him go if that was Hank Coldwell? He's a famous gunman, son. They say he's quite a vile killer. They wouldn't just turn a man like that loose."

"They probably didn't recognize him. And even if they did, there ain't no charges on him nowhere. He's so good that nobody's ever been able to pin a murder on him. The law knows he kills folks, but the only ones they can pin on him for sure have been self-defense. He's been tried three times for murder and cleared every time, even though everybody knows he's guilty as sin all three times."

"My son reads too many dime novels," Barger said to Liam. "Kenneth, meet Mr. Liam Carrigan."

Kenneth turned and nodded at Liam. "Hello, sir."

"Hello."

The boy continued to stare.

"Something wrong?" Liam asked.

"I seen you trying to go after Coldwell out there on the porch. Did you know who it was?"

"The name he told me was Murphy."

"Well, now that you know the truth, if I was you, I'd lay low after you get out of here. I wouldn't want to be the man who took a lunge at Hank Coldwell, no, sir."

"You ain't being polite, boy," said Henry Barger.

"Young fellow, just how sure are you that this fellow is Coldwell?" asked Liam.

"Completely sure, sir. I read about outlaws and gunfighters all the time. I collect wanted posters and cut stories out of newspapers. I've even got some actual pictures, took direct."

"It's the truth," admitted Barger. "The boy knows his criminals. It worries me sometimes that he's so interested in them."

"I'm interested because I want to be a lawman," Kenneth said.

"Tell me something," Liam said. "Do you know if Coldwell ever keeps company with a sort of weaselly fellow, dark hair, greasy look, whiskers, skinny build—"

"Sounds like Sam Leisure. I don't know for sure, though. Coldwell has ridden with several different folks. But that sure sounds like it could be Sam Leisure."

"If it is, he ain't much to write home about. I gave this fellow a scare on the porch of my hotel, and he ran like a chicken with a fox behind it."

"Sam Leisure is the nephew of Coldwell, the son of Coldwell's sister, who was murdered," Kenneth said with an air of professorial authority. "He's not nearly the man that his uncle is. The talk is he's a coward. But the talk also is that Coldwell is attached to him and won't work without him. There's also a rumor that after a bad wagon accident a few years ago that walloped him bad on the skull, Coldwell become prone to the fits. Seizes up and bites his tongue and jerks about and all that sometimes. Sam Leisure takes care of him when the fits strike him."

"Being prone to the fits could be quite a problem for a man who makes his living by a steady trigger finger," Liam observed.

"I was thinking the same," Henry said.

"Coldwell is primarily a gun for hire, if memory serves and what I've been told is correct," said Liam.

"Yes, mostly," Kenneth replied. "Though no one can ever prove it. Like I said, he's been cleared by every jury who ever heard a case against him."

Liam mulled some things over for a couple of moments. "I suppose a killer as good as Coldwell would cost a pretty penny to hire."

Kenneth nodded.

"So the kinds of men who could hire him could probably afford to buy off juries and prosecutors and judges, too."

"Why are you so interested in what my boy's saying, Mr. Carrigan?" Henry asked.

"I'm just trying to figure out all I can about a situation that my brother and I have run across."

"Your brother?"

"Yes. His name is Joseph, and he's in town here but has no notion I've been jailed." Liam paused as an inspiration struck. "Henry, I'd like to hire your fine son to do a job for me, if you and he are willing."

Henry looked very willing right away. "He'll do it," he said quickly.

"What is the job?" Kenneth asked.

"I want you to go find my brother and tell him where I am, and see if he can do anything to get me out of here. I'll give you three dollars if you'll bring him back here to me."

"How will I know him?"

Liam gave a thorough description of Joseph and told Kenneth in which portion of town he'd likely find him. "He's looking for someone himself just now, a young woman who is in a spot of trouble. There are others looking for her, too . . . in fact, the same men you say are Coldwell and Leisure."

Kenneth looked solemn all at once, and Henry's face lost all expression.

"If you don't want Kenneth to do this, I'll understand," Liam said to Henry. "I don't want to put the boy in any position of danger."

Henry pursed his lips. "Three dollars?"

"Make it four. And if he sees Coldwell or his partner—assuming that's who they really are—he needn't go through with it. I wouldn't have him get involved with killers, no matter how indirectly."

"It's a deal," Henry said. "Right, Kenneth?"

"Right," Kenneth replied, though with somewhat less enthusiasm than his father. Liam made a promise to himself that he'd hand the money directly to the boy, not to Henry on his behalf. Maybe Kenneth could get it spent or at least hidden before his father got out of jail to waste it on whiskey.

At Liam's request, Kenneth spat back Joseph's description for Liam's approval and went on his way. Henry stared at his jailmate with open curiosity.

"Let me ask you something. If Kenneth is right about who that man is, and if he really is after a young woman, what did she do to get such a wicked devil as Hank Coldwell on her trail?"

"I'm wondering the same thing. All I know about her is that she's carrying a baby in her. Makes you wonder if there's somebody who very much doesn't want to see that baby be born."

Henry's brows lowered and came together. "That's downright sad, thinking that somebody would want to do such a thing. It kind of reminds you of that story about that fellow in the Bible. Moses or somebody. The one that Egyptian fellow tried to kill when he was just a baby."

"We'll just hope that this baby proves out to be as lucky as Moses was," Liam said.

10

Lying on his back in the cellar of the ruined house, Joseph stared up through the hole in the floor. He felt quite numb, and feared for a second or two that he'd paralyzed himself. Then abruptly the numbness vanished, and he tried to groan but couldn't, because the breath had been so completely knocked out of him that he hadn't drawn a breath since impact. He felt wrenched and battered over every inch of his body, particularly the back side of it.

He wondered who had shoved him. The woman, probably—April McCree, unless he'd stumbled across a second auburn-haired young woman on the run in this little town, which didn't seem likely.

Suddenly her head appeared from above. Her face peered down through the hole in the stairs, auburn hair hanging down toward him. She squinted, trying to see him in what was from her perspective a dark pit.

"Who are you?" she demanded.

Joseph tried to speak, but his breath still failed him.

"For God's sake, why can't you leave me in peace? Why are you so determined to kill me?"

He knew then that she thought he was one of her pursuers.

She raised her head suddenly, looking down the staircase into the house. Joseph heard a noise, muffled, as if of someone moving about in the house's main level. She wheeled and vanished up the stairs.

Joseph's head was spinning; he struggled to draw in air, beginning to be terrified by his inability to do so, and finally, *finally* was able to pull in a large gasp. He wheezed loudly, drinking in precious air. At the same moment something moved across the hole in the stairs, a male figure partly striding and partly leaping across it, going up the stairs after the young woman.

Joseph pushed himself up and stared through the openings above him. He had to get up there, but to do that he first had to get out of the cellar.

He looked about in the relative darkness for an exit. He saw a staircase leading up to a door on the first floor, but the staircase was mostly gone, just a pile of rubble.

Above he heard the shout of a male, saying something he couldn't make out, then footsteps pounding about, hard enough that he could hear them clearly even though they were two levels above him.

Then she screamed, and Joseph went weak in the knees.

He clambered onto the heaped rubble that once was a staircase and struggled to climb toward the door. It was difficult given his injured hand and soreness from his fall.

Above, another scream, another shout from an angry male voice, and a terrible sound of knocking and thumping, something thudding hard to the floor . . .

Joseph had reached the base of the door when the remnants of the staircase gave way. He fell amid lumber and grit and dust and splinters back down to the cellar floor, rubble piling atop him. For a moment he was stunned, but he'd avoided having his breath knocked out of him and quickly recovered.

Pushing aside the wood, he extricated himself from the pile, coughing in the dust and airborne mold. Above, the struggle was still going strong, and seemed to be louder, as if those involved were working their way closer to the main staircase above.

Joseph looked around for something he could use as a climbing pole or ladder or any other contrivance that might get him to that door. He laid a long plank from the staircase at a slant up to the door and climbed it. He reached the base of the door, reached up, almost had his hand toward the latch . . .

It was just out of reach.

The woman screamed again, then there was a hard, dull, cracking sound, a loud grunt, and the sound of something dropping to the floor.

Then silence. The battle upstairs had come to a sudden end.

Joseph closed his eyes. Too late.

He had failed her.

While Henry Barger snored on his bunk, Liam paced in his cell, mind working hard, playing a game of "what if" with the few solid facts that he possessed.

Liam didn't know how much credence to put in what Kenneth Barger had said. He was just a boy, obsessed for whatever reason with outlawry, maybe spouting more fantasies than fact. But what if he was right, and the man whom Liam had met as "Murphy" really was Hank Coldwell, infamous hired killer? What if?

Liam lined up the few things he knew. The first was that April McCree was indeed being pursued by "Murphy," or Coldwell, or whoever he was, and the weaselly fellow who worked with him. If Murphy really was Coldwell, and assuming he wasn't pursuing her for personal reasons but working as usual on behalf of someone with the means to hire him, that meant that April McCree had an enemy of some stature.

That alone told him very little. But there was one further fact, something April had said to him in the hotel room: She'd told him that she'd come to his room not at random, but because she'd seen the name "Carrigan" on the register. The Carrigan name had meant something to her . . . but unfortunately the Weasel had appeared at the window at that moment and she'd not had the opportunity to tell Liam what that meaning was.

Liam took a hypothetical leap: What if the reason she responded to the Carrigan name was because she'd known Patrick Carrigan—not the one who was Liam and Joseph's uncle, but the unfortunate traveling fighter who had been hauled off and killed on the plains? What if?

If so, then it seemed a likely bet that Patrick Carrigan had been taken out on the plains and killed by the same people who now pursued April McCree.

But why? How could a young couple have earned themselves so fearsome an enemy? And who could be so hardened as to send a hired killer after a young pregnant woman, for any reason?

Then the last leap, the biggest "What If?" of all: What if the slain Pat Carrigan was connected with Liam and Joseph's uncle . . . a son, perhaps? If so, this whole affair suddenly became very close to the hearts of Liam and Joseph Carrigan. It would make the slain Patrick Carrigan their own cousin. It would establish a strong tie between their family and poor April McCree.

It was hard to believe it had all started with Joseph's sleepy glimpse of a sign being burned in a small town back lot.

Liam hoped that Joseph would find April McCree. Theories and guesses were one thing, but he wanted solid answers. And those could only be provided by April McCree herself.

11

Joseph, unable to reach the latch, had lowered himself to floor level again, and looked up through the holes in the floor and staircase into the now-silent house above him. But not entirely silent.

Footfalls, descending the top of the staircase, softly and slowly.

Joseph drew his pistol and waited.

A face appeared, looking down at him. Joseph was so astonished that he almost dropped his pistol. It was the young woman!

"I see you down there!" she said in a trembling voice. "I'll kill you, too, just like I killed your partner! I've got his pistol now, and I'll use it!"

Good Lord, she'd *killed* the man who attacked her?

"Wait!" Joseph said. "Wait, I'm not who you think I am! Don't shoot!"

"Are you the one who has been chasing me?"

"No, I'm not. I swear it!"

"I don't believe you! I believe you're *him!*"

"Wait . . . wait. I'll let you see my face. You'll see I'm not who you think." Joseph quietly holstered his pistol, reached into his pocket, pulled out a block of matches, snapped two off, and lit both. He held them so that the flames illuminated his face from the side, and looked up at her.

"Oh, merciful God!" she exclaimed, leaping to her feet, leaping across the hole in the stairs and going down to the main floor.

Joseph shook out the matches, perplexed. Why had she reacted so strongly just at seeing the face of a stranger?

He heard her run across the floor, somewhat haphazardly, as if she did not know exactly where to go, but then she veered toward the door to the cellar, and the latch rattled.

The door swung open.

"Don't step down—no stairs!" Joseph called.

The warning came just in time. She actually lunged out into the open space but caught herself on the doorframe and pulled back to safety.

"Dear God!" she said in a whisper, shaken by what had nearly happened. She pulled back away from the door, but quickly reappeared.

"I'll find you something to climb on!" she called down, and vanished again from the doorway.

It took a couple of minutes, but she returned and

thrust an honest-to-goodness ladder down through the door. "I found this lying in the back of the house," she explained.

The ladder could not properly stand because the rubble was in the way. It took two minutes of struggling and moving lumber to get it into a usable position. Joseph mounted it with trepidation—it was rickety and old—but it held him as he climbed, and he reached the door safely and stepped through it.

"I've never seen so deep a cellar," he said to the young woman he was seeing clearly for the first time in his life.

What he saw was a face that was every bit as beautiful as Liam had said, but at the moment darkened by disappointment.

"You thought I was someone else," he said to her as he brushed dust and grit off his clothing.

"Yes . . . I'm sorry. You sound so much like him, and your face, your eyes . . . so much the same. But I knew it couldn't be. He's gone. I'll not ever see him again."

Joseph was eager to talk with her at length, find out whom she was talking about and all the details of her story, but now was not the time. "Is there a dead man upstairs?" he asked.

"Yes. I killed him. I didn't really mean to . . . I was just defending myself."

"Show him to me."

She led Joseph up the stairs—with great care he crossed the hole through which he'd already fallen once—and led him around to what had once been a bedroom. On the dirty and uneven floor lay the body of a thin, dirty, long-haired man. Literally nailed to his head was a board that had a nail through it nearly the size of a spike. It protruded into his temple.

"You hit him with the board," Joseph said.

"Yes. I didn't even know there was a nail. It sank into his temple, and he fell like he'd just suddenly turned to a wet rag."

Joseph knelt, examined the wound, and felt the chest just to make sure there was no heartbeat. There wasn't. He stood.

"Do you know him?"

"I don't know his name. He is one of two men who have been following me. They want to kill me. They've already killed the man I was going to marry."

"Why?"

"It's a long story. Suffice it to say that my existence is a problem for someone who can't afford a problem right now."

"We've got to go to the law, you know."

"No! No . . . if you do that, he'll find me!"

"Who is 'he'?"

"The one who is the partner of this one." She gestured at the corpse. "I don't know his name, either.

He's older, bigger than this one. His eyes are frightening to see. Evil."

"Am I correct to assume that you are April McCree?"

Her eyes widened in that stunning but drawn face, and she took a step back. "How do you know me?"

"I had a good description of you from Liam Carrigan, whom you met when you hid in his hotel room."

The fear in her expression deepened, and she backed away all the way to the wall. "I only took the money because I was desperate! I still have most of it . . . I'll give it back to you! Please, just let me go!"

"The money isn't the issue. Liam won that at a poker table, and he doesn't care that you took it. He's worried about you. He wants to find you and help you. I'm his brother, so I've been looking for you today, too."

"You're his brother . . . so you also are a Carrigan . . ."

"Yes."

She gazed at him closely, her eyes filling with tears. "I knew it—you are so much like him!"

"People do tell me that Liam and I bear a strong resemblance."

"No, not your brother . . . you look so very much like—"

Noise, downstairs. Someone had just entered the house. Joseph lifted a finger to his lips, but it was not necessary. She'd quit speaking the instant they heard the front door creak.

Joseph and April looked at one another, sharing the same thought: If they moved, they risked revealing their presence, because in this damaged, skewed structure, every movement caused creakings and snappings. But if they did not move, and whoever that was came up the stairs, they would be found . . . standing over a dead body.

Joseph knew he had to get them out of there. A pregnant young woman, two men, one of them dead, an isolated and unlikely location—this had all the look of a romantic triangle gone bad and devolved into murder.

"Try to move quietly," Joseph said. "The window . . . and wait, take this . . ." He quietly extracted from his pocket a key to his and Liam's hotel room, the same one in which she'd hidden. Joseph had obtained a key for himself when he and Liam had decided to linger in Culpepperville to search for April. "Please be careful," he whispered. "Liam told me you said you were with child."

She took the key and moved gingerly toward the window. Three steps in that direction, and the floor creaked.

Whoever was moving around downstairs stopped moving. She looked back over her shoulder at Joseph and winced. He motioned for her to keep going.

She reached the window without much further noise, but it was closed. As she raised it, it made a racket. The footsteps below resumed, heading quickly toward the staircase.

She put a leg out the window, then the other, stepping onto the roof of the back porch. Pulling her ragged and filthy skirts out after her, she vanished from Joseph's sight. He wondered if she was trapped on the porch roof or would find a way down. He hoped she would not take a desperate leap in her condition.

He carried on a fast debate in his mind. He could go out the window himself and try to escape. Or, he could do to whoever was climbing the stairs essentially the same thing that April had done to him. He could rush out, kick the intruder back down the stairs, and let him fall into the cellar through the gap in the staircase.

But what if it was a lawman? What if it was Liam? Or the owner of this ruined house, come to investigate a report of intruders? Or just an inquisitive individual poking around an old abandoned dwelling?

Joseph couldn't risk hurting an innocent individual. Nor could he risk being found in the same room as a dead man.

Joseph chose the window. There was no longer any point in worrying about making noise. He ran to the window and climbed out of it. April was not on the porch roof. He spotted the top edge of a trellis extending up past the roofline and climbed upon it as she evidently had before him. But he was heavier than she, and the trellis pulled loose from the porch and tilted back with him, dumping him onto the ground.

He hit hard, and it hurt, especially given that he had to catch part of his weight on his splinted hand. These were hard-battering times for Joseph Carrigan: a train crash, a fall into a deep cellar, and now a plunge onto the ground aboard a tilting trellis.

He was just coming to his feet when he heard the roar of a male voice through the window he'd just exited. The body had been found, and given the emotion that registered in the animal cry echoing out the window, the finder knew the one murdered and was reacting with pain and fury.

So it had to be the other man pursuing April, the one who had come to the doorway of Liam's hotel room.

Joseph ran toward a nearby woodshed, hoping to hide behind it before the second man came to the window. It would be far easier to evade him if the man didn't know what Joseph looked like.

But a tree root had other plans. He tripped over it and sprawled, just as the man appeared at the window. Joseph reflexively looked back, then cursed at himself at once for having done so. The man was leaning out the window, glaring at him, face twisted in fury.

"You!" the man shouted. "Was it you who did this?"

Joseph wasn't about to pin the blame where it really lay. The man was already trying to kill April, and giving him an even stronger motive would not help her at all.

"I didn't kill him. I found him there, already dead," Joseph said, coming to his feet. "I don't know who killed him."

"Who the hell are you?"

"An innocent man." Joseph's eyes flicked from side to side, looking for April and hoping he did not see her. He hoped she was far away, out of sight and making distance.

He would keep this conversation engaged, if he could, and give her more time.

That ambition became instantly pointless. A movement in the trees caught his eye and also that of the man in the window. Joseph's heart sank as he saw the edge of April's dress peeking out from behind a tree. She'd not run, merely hidden.

The man in the window said, "I see you, whore! Was it you who did this?"

Joseph said, "She didn't do it! I admit it . . . it was me!"

"I'll kill you both!" the man said, and vanished from the window.

12

Joseph shouted to April, "Run! He's coming . . ."

She ran back into the trees, pausing one moment to look back piteously at him, then continuing as he waved her on.

Joseph himself ran in the opposite direction, around the back of the shed and toward a field overgrown with saplings and brush. His idea was to remain visible enough to draw the pursuer after him and not April, but to maintain enough cover between himself and the man to make it unlikely he'd be able to get off a good shot at him.

If need be, Joseph would defend himself with lethal force. But he hesitated to do so. He was no killer by nature, despite having fought in the war. More importantly, he did not know much about April McCree or why she was pursued. His every instinct spoke in her favor, rousing in him protectiveness and the presumption that she was being victimized. Yet perhaps she was not what she appeared.

She'd violently killed a man within the last few minutes, albeit in clear self-defense . . . but in some prior circumstance might she have been a killer of an entirely different type? Might the men pursuing her be doing so for good and righteous reasons?

He ran through the saplings and brush, looking behind him, watching for pursuit. But there was none. He stopped, a bad feeling creeping over him.

"Come get me, you bastard!" he called. "I'll kill you like I killed your partner!"

No response. The wind rustled the trees.

Joseph knew he'd made a dreadful error of judgment. His ploy hadn't worked. Either the man had pursued neither of them, or he was pursuing April.

Joseph should have engaged him in a gunfight, or gone around to intercept him as he left the house . . . anything to make sure he didn't pursue April McCree.

Furious at himself, Joseph turned and hurried back toward the lot, keeping low in case his foe was anticipating just such a move and waited to pick him off. Joseph kept his pistol ready just in case.

When he reached the lot, behind the house, and explored around and in the shed and in every place someone might hide, he realized that he really was alone. He began looking for tracks or any other evidence the man might have gone into the woods after April.

He found footmarks, the heel depressions cut in deeply as they would be if left by a running man. He followed them into the woods, wondering if he'd already caught her and what he might be doing to her.

Joseph plunged deeper into the woods, following the tracks until they reached stony ground and were lost. At that point he looked around, trying to surmise which way she might have run. He was encouraged that, at the very least, he hadn't heard any shots, any yells or screams. She was young and strong, the other man middle-aged and much heavier. Maybe she'd outrun him!

Joseph was just south of town, within stone-throwing distance of the most outlying buildings and nearly within reach of the back lots of the store buildings and houses fronting one of the larger streets. Maybe she'd gone in that direction. Sometimes it was safer to hide among people than alone in an empty place. Yes, that was what she'd have done. No one could murder a young woman in the middle of a town street, in open daylight.

He holstered his pistol, hiding it under his coat, then paused a moment to readjust the splints on his left hand, wincing and biting his lip at the pain. Then he took a deep breath and headed north, into town.

Hank Coldwell stepped out of the alley and received a sound bump as someone of small stature walked right into him.

Hank Coldwell's icy eyes stared down into the eyes

of the boy who had just collided with him. "Learn to watch where you're going, boy!"

The boy's mouth hung open, his eyes wide and unblinking. He backed away, tripped on his own heels, and fell on his rump. Then words came out that he regretted at once. "I'm sorry, Mr. Coldwell."

Coldwell raised a brow. The boy knew him! "What did you call me?"

"I . . . I . . ."

"It so happens my name is Murphy."

"Yes, sir, Mr. Murphy."

"Why'd you call me that name?"

"It's just that . . . I read about . . . I'm interested in . . . I've got pictures of . . ." He couldn't finish.

"You ain't been following me, have you, boy?"

"No sir, no sir . . . I ain't. I'm just out looking for another man, sir. His brother is in the jail and sent me out to find him so he could spring him."

"The jail . . ."

"Yes, sir."

"I was in that jail until this morning."

"Yes, sir. My father's in there, too." Kenneth Barger's voice was quaking.

"Is your father the drunk who was in the cell across from me?"

Kenneth lowered his face a little. "Yes."

Coldwell lifted one brow slightly. "Talkative man. Annoyed me."

"My pap talks too much, Mr. Murphy."

"You're respectful. I like that in a boy. Yeah, I remember you now. You were in there talking to your father. You kept looking over at me. I guess you thought I was this Coldwell fellow. I think there's a rather famous gunman by that name."

"Yes, sir. I've seen camera pictures of him. You're . . . I mean, he's very famous."

"Tell me something, boy: Have you seen a woman coming through town anywhere, darkish hair, big eyes, dressed ragged and dirty . . . probably running or acting sneakish?"

"No, sir."

"Yeah. Well, if you do, and if you see me, you let me know. I need to find that woman."

"Yes, sir."

Coldwell started to turn away, then stopped and faced Kenneth again. "Hold on, son. If your father is the cell across from the one I was in, then the one who sent you looking for his brother must be the fellow they took into jail as I was going out."

"Yes, sir. He's in the cell you was in."

"That man threatened me. Tried to pull away from the lawmen and get at me. He was a fellow I saw once before that. I believe he may have given refuge last night to the very woman I'm trying to find." Coldwell pulled a cigar from his pocket and bit the end off it. "That woman's hard to catch. I been

trying for a good while now. Mighty hard to catch."
He struck a match and lit the cigar. "You know the
name of the man in the cell, boy?"

"Yes, sir. It's Liam Carrigan."

"Carrigan!"

"Yes, sir."

Coldwell drew on the cigar and blew out a stream
of smoke. "I ran into a Carrigan once before. Over at
Hooper. He was a fighter, quite a scrapper. I took a lit-
tle trip out onto the plains with that particular Mr.
Carrigan. Special little trip." He paused. "This Liam
Carrigan in the jail has a brother, you say."

"That's right. His name is Joseph."

Coldwell took another thoughtful drag and
watched the smoke disperse as he blew it out. "I'm
doing some thinking here, son. The Carrigan I met
over in Hooper was what you might call a mighty
close friend of the woman I'm looking for. Then this
Liam Carrigan fellow gave refuge to the same woman.
So maybe there's a whole clan of these Carrigans, and
they all are tied in with this woman. Tell me what
Joseph Carrigan looks like, son."

"Well, I ain't seen him myself, but his brother gave
me a description." Kenneth passed that description
on to Coldwell.

Coldwell chuckled around the end of his cigar. "I
believe I saw Joseph Carrigan, this very day. But I lost
him. I'd sure like to find him again. How much is Liam

Carrigan paying you to bring his brother to him?"

"Four dollars."

"You bring him to me instead, and I'll give you ten."

"Ten dollars!"

"That's right."

"Where would I find you, sir, if'n I did see him or the woman?"

"I've got a room in a boardinghouse over on Stewart Street. Yellow paint on the clapboards."

"I know the place, sir."

"Can you write?"

"Yes, sir."

"If you don't find me there, you write me a note and seal it up. Leave it with the landlady. My name is Murphy. Murphy. You understand me?"

"Yes, sir."

"Don't ever use that other name you called when you're talking about me. You understand? And, boy . . . don't you do a thing to cause me a problem. You won't cause me a problem, will you, boy?"

"No, sir."

"Good."

"Sir, Mr. Murphy . . . are you alone? Ain't there somebody maybe who is kind of a partner to you?"

Coldwell's face lost all expression. "There was. Not anymore. Sorry to say it."

He threw down his cigar and walked away.

13

Taking back routes, staying as out of view of the main thoroughfares as he could, Joseph reached the hotel. He had seen neither April nor the man chasing her. He hoped to heaven that it didn't mean the man had caught her in some hidden location and done her in.

He entered the hotel and climbed the stairs. At the door of his room he knocked. No answer from within. "It's me," he said through the door. "April, if you're in there, you can let me in."

Nothing.

Joseph left the hotel and climbed the exterior staircase up to the third-level porch. He went to the window of the room and looked through a gap in the curtains. The room was empty. He tried to raise the window, hoping nobody was looking, but it was locked.

He wasn't sure what to do next. Probably try to

find Liam, who most likely was still searching his side of town. The thought of Liam brought a sudden concern. If Liam had found April, then her pursuer might find Liam as well.

Joseph descended to the street and headed toward the north end of town.

Hank Coldwell rounded a corner and saw her. Her back toward him, she moved along quickly, not quite running but walking in the manner of someone hurrying for shelter as a storm rolls in.

He smiled and gave a quick nod of satisfaction. At last, a chance to end the assignment. Following her dark and shadowed trail had taken far too long and required too much effort. It should have been much easier than it had been to deal with a terrified woman who had the mischance to make an enemy of the wrong man.

As of today, however, the task of dealing with April McCree had a whole new meaning. Now it was personal. The loss of his nephew demanded revenge, and he would extract it from the girl herself and the two Carrigan brothers, who had emerged from nowhere to interfere with his business.

Joseph Carrigan would pay the steepest price. It was he, Coldwell believed, who had actually killed his nephew.

Thoughts of Sam lying dead back in that empty

house were enough to moisten Coldwell's eyes. Sam Leisure had never been much help to Coldwell—too much of a coward when the pressure got high—but he'd been family. The only family Coldwell had left, the son of a beloved sister whose death he could still barely acknowledge. And Sam had been helpful indeed in those dreaded but fortunately rare times that the fits seized hold of Coldwell. At those times the feared killer was like a helpless and pitiful infant, but Sam never laughed, never looked down on him. He held him, talked comfort to him, kept him from injuring himself, told him everything would be fine in just a moment.

Now he was gone. Coldwell wiped away a tear and cursed the Carrigan brothers and April McCree.

Coldwell watched her step onto a boardwalk and hurry toward a shabby two-story building about a block ahead. A boardinghouse, he suspected. But she went on past it and turned out of sight down an alley.

He headed across the street and went after her. At the head of the alley, he paused, glanced around the corner, then advanced.

When he reached the end of the alley he saw her entering the picket-fenced yard of a small shack, apparently a residence. That struck him as odd; how could such a transient as April McCree have residence in what looked like a permanent dwelling?

He had taken his first step to follow her into the yard when he was hit by what felt like a falling chimney. He fell hard, the wind crushed out of his lungs. Something pounded his jaw, and he realized that what had hit him was a human being, running and hitting at full force.

The blow to his jaw stunned Coldwell and actually blurred his vision for a moment. Through a foggy haze he saw the face of a man he'd last seen in the back lot of the house where Sam had died.

Coldwell came up with a knee and caught Joseph inside the thigh. An upward shove, and Joseph Carrigan was off and on the ground.

Coldwell sprang up with astonishing lightness for a man of his age and size. As he did, he saw the girl in her yard, watching aghast as the two men fought within yards of her.

It wasn't April McCree. Coldwell might have cursed or might have laughed, had he had a moment to do either.

Coldwell kicked Joseph, aiming for the ribs, but Joseph rolled and the blow merely glanced off, scuffing across his side. Coldwell lost his balance, staggered backward, tripped, and fell against the wall.

Joseph came up and struck Coldwell in the jaw, staggering him. Coldwell reached for his pistol. He heard the woman in the yard of the little house scream, and from the corner of his eye saw her run inside.

Coldwell took a kick in the knee from his opponent. His leg gave way.

Coldwell raised the pistol, cursing. Joseph put his shoulder down and charged, hitting Coldwell in the belly and crushing him against the wall behind him.

Coldwell almost lost his pistol. Joseph grabbed Coldwell's wrist and shoved it back against the wall. The pistol dropped. Joseph swept his splinted hand down, shoveled up the pistol on his palm, and threw it high in the air. It landed on the roof of the building behind him and stayed there.

Coldwell cursed and groped for a small knife sheathed on his belt. Joseph rocked his chin with another blow, then swung his elbow around to hit him on the side of the head.

Coldwell came up with his knife and slashed. It clipped a cuff button off the sleeve of Joseph's coat. Coldwell slashed again and nicked Joseph in the arm. Joseph hit him twice in the face, stunning him.

A man appeared at the end of the alley, watched for a moment, then ran away.

Joseph and Coldwell continued to grapple, Coldwell slashing, Joseph dodging. At last, over the noise of their fighting, Coldwell heard the thump of approaching footsteps, someone running toward them. Time to go. He dodged Joseph's last blow, shoved him down, then turned and ran.

Joseph, seated, leaned back against the wall, reached down and flipped the holding strap off the hammer of his pistol. He drew it, aimed it at the fleeing Coldwell, and hollered for him to stop. Coldwell kept going, dodged around a corner and out of sight.

"Drop the pistol, friend!" a voice called from the far end of the alley.

A man with a badge was edging toward Joseph, pistol out and gripped in both hands, cocked and ready to fire.

"He's getting away!" Joseph said.

"Who?"

"Him . . . that man . . ."

"I don't know who you're talking about. There's no man here now. But I know there's a gun law in this town and a law against brawling, and you're in violation of both! Drop the pistol, or I swear I'll shoot off your hand!"

Joseph lowered the pistol and laid it aside, on the ground.

"Kick it out of reach," the deputy ordered, still advancing.

Joseph obeyed.

"Come on," the deputy said. "You and me are going to make a visit to the jail."

Joseph stood slowly, feeling battered and stiff as an old man. "Listen, sir, there's a young woman who was being pursued by a man intent on killing her. I saw her, and saw him following, and I attacked him to protect her. Her name is April McCree, and she's in that house there. Ask her! She'll tell you what I was doing. She'll speak for me."

"Hands up, straight up, like you're trying to touch the moon! Now!"

Joseph obeyed, standing there feeling foolish. The deputy kept the pistol trained on him and glanced toward the little house.

The door opened and a young woman emerged. It was not April McCree.

"Ma'am, do you know this man?" the deputy asked.

"No," she said.

"Were you aware of anyone following you, either this man or another?"

"No."

"Is your name April McCree?"

"No."

The deputy looked at Joseph like a man would look at a piece of spoiled meat. "Let's you and me take a walk to the jail, my friend. What's your name, by the way?"

Joseph was in the foulest of humors. "Thomas Jefferson," he said.

The deputy apparently didn't catch the sarcasm. "All right, Mr. Jefferson. Let's go put you where you can't cause any more trouble. Step fast!"

14

Liam lay again on his miserable jailhouse bunk, staring up at the crossed, flat, iron bars above him, his fingers interlocked behind his neck.

Obviously something had not gone right with young Kenneth Barger's search for Joseph. It had been hours, and the boy hadn't returned. Liam had given up on him. Henry Barger, now freed, had taken it badly. The loss of four dollars pained him greatly. When a jailer showed up to turn Henry loose, Liam had the jailer bring him three dollars from his personal effects stowed up in the marshal's office and give them to Henry, just to keep him from taking out his disappointment on his son.

At length Liam went to sleep, arm stretched across his eyes. He woke up but did not rise when the deputy brought in a new prisoner and ensconced him in the cell that had been vacated by Henry Barger.

"There you go, Mr. Jefferson," Liam heard the

deputy say. "Get in there and settle yourself down."

"Jefferson" merely grunted in response. When the cell door was locked, he began to pace back and forth.

Liam tried to fall asleep again, but the pacing annoyed him. He sat up.

"For mercy's sake, friend, would you sit down and—" He cut off.

Joseph turned and gaped. "Liam?"

"Good Lord, brother! What are you doing in there!"

"I'd like to ask you the same."

"I was arrested for attacking a man who I thought was the skinny fellow who was out on the hotel porch. And for carrying a pistol within the city limits."

"I was arrested for brawling and carrying a pistol."

"Brawling? Joseph Carrigan was brawling?"

Joseph came to his cell door and motioned for Liam to do the same.

"Liam, there's some serious things I have to tell you."

"I've got some serious news for you, too, Joseph. Like the fact that one of the two fellows chasing April McCree is Hank Coldwell. Yes, the one you've heard of."

Joseph felt a little weak. "Are you sure? The hired killer?"

"That's right. And they say he comes expensive. Which means that whoever is after April is somebody with a lot of money."

"Liam, it was Coldwell that I was brawling with. I saw him trailing a woman I thought was April McCree, and I attacked him to protect her."

"And you lived to tell me about it."

"Yes. I guess I'm lucky, huh?"

"Attacking Hank Coldwell? Yeah, I'd say you're lucky."

"Listen, Liam: I found her."

"April McCree?"

"Yes . . . I found her, and had a chance to talk to her a little. But we were forced apart, and I've not been able to find her again."

"Is she all right?"

"I don't know. I hope so. Liam, there's a dead body in the mix now. The fellow on the hotel porch . . . dead now."

"You killed him?"

"I told Coldwell that it was me, but I only said that to protect her. She did it, Liam. She hit him in the head with a board that had a big nail sticking out of it—it sank into his temple and killed him deader than stone."

Liam whistled beneath his breath. "Sounds like you've got a story to tell. Go ahead and tell it."

Joseph did, as succinctly as possible, telling Liam

everything that had happened and everything that April had told him. And it was then that he spoke with obvious frustration, because the appearance of Coldwell had cut short so much more that she would have revealed.

Liam told his own tale, then, passing on what Kenneth Barger had declared and his hiring of the boy to find Joseph.

"He didn't find me," Joseph said. "I saw no sign of such a boy."

"I suppose he gave up, then. Joseph, we've got to get out of here. We've got to find her. She'll be dead as soon as Coldwell gets to her."

"All right. Is there a bail we can pay? Some way to break out of here?"

"I don't know. Let's talk to the jailer. Tell him we want a lawyer, maybe."

"Want me to holler for him, 'Mr. Jefferson'?"

"Go ahead."

"What's the Jefferson business about, anyway?"

"Nothing. Just a joke that got taken seriously."

The jailer came promptly after being called, though he seemed not happy to be bothered. "You'll get your supper at six o'clock," the jailer said before they had time to speak. "We got us a woman who cooks it and brings it over."

"It's not supper I want to talk about," Liam said, "I need to find out what I have to do to get out of here.

I've not seen a judge, had a lawyer come by, nothing. I want to see a judge, or I want out of here."

"You'll be out soon enough."

"How soon?"

"In the morning. I was told to let you out before breakfast."

"What about me?" Joseph asked.

"Tomorrow afternoon."

"Is this the way you do law in this town? Lock folks up with no trial, no lawyer, then just turn them loose after they've been in for so long?"

"I'm just the jailer. I do what I'm told."

"I'd like to get out tonight, right now," Liam said. "I've been here all day, and I've got a little sister and old grandmother camped outside town waiting for me to come back and take care of them, and they don't even know where I am. Let me go . . . and let my friend Mr. Jefferson over there go, too, if you would."

The jailer laughed. He glanced over at Joseph, then back at Liam. "You know, you two sort of look alike. Look alike a whole lot, in fact."

"Let us go, come on."

"Can't."

"Are you open to bribes?"

A long pause. But then a shake of the head. "Not me, friend. Not me. You just settle down and be patient."

"Let us out!"

"Can't."

"Liam."

"Hmm?"

Joseph thumped the well-gnawed chicken bone on his tin plate. Nothing remained of supper but a couple of bites of biscuit and a fragment of potato. Liam had made even quicker work of his supper and now sat back on his bunk, feet crossed before him.

"I'm concerned about something I did today. I did it thinking it best at the time, but now I believe it was a mistake."

"What was that?"

"I gave April McCree my key to the hotel room."

Liam thought about that. "And you're thinking that might be a dangerous place for her to go. Because Hank Coldwell knows where it is."

"You told me that he saw her handkerchief on your floor. He knows she was there."

"And he knows I'm here, too. He saw me being taken in . . . I guess I made that pretty much a certainty by trying to go after him like I did."

"He could come after you here, Liam."

"Why would he do that? He wants her, not me. But it might cross his mind to look at the hotel again."

"She'll be too smart to go there. I hope."

"So do I."

• • •

Clouds obscured the moon, and to the good fortune of Hank Coldwell, the hotel was mostly empty. Not a single light burned in any window on the third floor. As he moved down the porch toward the window that led into the room where he'd encountered Liam Carrigan, he did so in total darkness.

Few people moved on the street below, and even if one should chance to look up and see him on the porch, it wouldn't be a problem. People relaxed on this porch all the time.

He reached the window and positioned himself beside it, leaning back against the wall, looking as nonchalant as possible. No attempt to hide himself; the point was to look as if there was no reason for him not to be where he was.

Below on the far side of the street, a man walked by, whistling and tapping his cane on the boardwalk. He did not look up. When he was gone, the street was empty.

Coldwell took off his coat, put it against the window, and broke out the center pane. With the coat to muffle it, there was hardly any sound. The pane fell inward and clattered on the floor, but there was no one but Coldwell himself to hear it.

He reached through the broken window and flipped the latch. The window went up, Coldwell went in.

128

He struck a match, found the lamp, and lit it. But by now he knew his effort was futile. She was not there.

He looked under the bed, in the wardrobe, and opened the door to peer into the hallway. Empty all around.

He cursed softly. He'd figured this would be a waste of time, but on the slender chance she would be foolish enough to try to hide in Carrigan's room, it had seemed worth a look.

He left the room the way he'd come and descended to the street. For tonight he'd give up on April McCree. He knew he'd not find her. But there was one other option open to him that might save the night from being a waste. He was determined to get rid of the Carrigan brothers. Joseph in particular, as the killer of Sam, but the other one as well. Liam, that was the name. The one in the jail earlier that day . . . and maybe still there tonight.

He pulled a cigar from his pocket, fired it up, and began striding in the direction of the jail.

He'd just turned a corner and gone out of sight when April McCree stepped out of the shadows on the far side of the street from the hotel. She stole across the street and climbed the outer staircase to the highest porch, then went down to the window that she'd watched Hank Coldwell break and open. She slid it up and went inside.

She would light no lamp; she dared not. But she would rest, and wait, and hope that either or both of the Carrigan brothers showed up. She did not know where they were or why they were not in their room now, and it was their absence, revealed by the darkness of the window, that had kept her from entering the room earlier. That, and the helpful voice of a warning instinct that told her her pursuer might look for her at the hotel tonight. She was glad she'd listened to it.

She felt safe nowhere these days, but in the Carrigans' room she felt more secure than she had at any other place for a long time. The phantom who tracked her would not return tonight, not if she kept the light off. She could eat of the bread she'd bought at a bakery, paid for with some of the money she'd taken from the bedside table in this very room. Then she could rest, for the sake of herself and her baby.

The few possessions that were April McCree's were in a cloth sack that closed with a long rope strap. This she typically wore tied around her waist, the bag on one hip.

Taking off the bag, she laid it on the bed and from it removed the pistol she had taken from the man she'd killed. Huddling with it, curling up in nearly a fetal position, she lay on the bed and wept from pure weariness and fear until she finally went to sleep.

15

The store had just closed when Hank Coldwell stepped onto the porch. The storekeeper was at the door, turning a key in the lock, and was startled when he turned to find Coldwell behind him.

"Evening, sir," Coldwell said.

"Hello. How are you?"

"I'd be much better if I could buy some coal oil."

"Sir, I just closed my doors."

"Surely you can help out one last customer. I'd like to buy two kegs of coal oil."

"Well, we stayed open late already. I hate to open up again at this hour."

"I think you can do it. Don't you?"

The man looked at Coldwell's piercing eyes and the rumpled and dirty state of his clothing, remnants of the earlier alleyway fight. He nodded. "I guess it's not a particular problem to help out one more customer."

The key went back into the lock. Hank Coldwell said, "Your cooperation is much appreciated, sir."

By the time Coldwell hauled the coal oil kegs all the way to the south side of town, he was exhausted. The kegs, though relatively small, were heavy. As soon as he was through the door of the wind-ruined and empty house, he gratefully set the kegs on the floor, collapsed, and rested for several minutes. The interior of the house was almost as dark as a cave, and there was no sound except the skittering of mice and the flappings of nesting birds.

Coldwell rose, picked up one of the kegs, and walked carefully across the dark room to the stairs. He climbed a short distance, then lit a match just long enough to identify the location of the gap in the stairs. He carefully stepped across it, then continued to the room where his slain nephew lay.

There was a bit of moonlight coming through the window. Coldwell set down the keg and walked over to the dead body. Sitting on the floor beside it, he pulled his knees up toward his chest and rested his chin on them, staring at the corpse. He began to weep, letting the tears flow freely.

"Sam, I'm sorry," he said. "I'll kill the bastards who did this to you, I vow. I'll make them pay. I only wish we'd stayed together today, and you hadn't come up here alone. I'm sorry."

132

He wept a while longer. "I'm glad your mother can't see what's happened here, Sam. I'm glad she can't know how I've failed to protect you." He rubbed his eyes. "I miss her, Sam. She was the finest person ever I knew. I'm sorry that she's gone, and that you are, too. You tell her I love her, will you? Tell her for me."

He sat without words for another five minutes, then stood and got the keg. Opening it, he poured coal oil over Sam's body and all around, draining the last of the coal oil down the stairs to the edge of the hole. He returned to the room long enough to pile loose pieces of wood, broken furniture, and the like, around and atop the body.

"I'm sorry, Sam," he said. "I wish I could let you have a real funeral and a proper burial. But I can't. We just can't have a lot of questions being asked about a dead man right now. And there's a good chance that somebody would figure I killed you. I just don't have time for that. I hope you'd understand. We'll let you go out all glorious instead, eh? All glorious and blazing."

Coldwell returned to the stairs, lit the line of coal oil, and watched the flames climb up and around the corner.

Coldwell went downstairs, fetched the other keg of coal oil, and left the house in a hurry. Going to a hidden place, he lingered long enough to make sure the fire had caught. The house, once fully engaged, would be an inferno that would thoroughly consume the body of Sam Leisure. If any traces were ever found at all, he would be unidentifiable. The assumption would be made that he was merely a drunken vagrant and probably started the fire himself, by accident.

When it was evident that the house was indeed going to burn, Coldwell continued across town. He had one more stop to make, one more fire to set.

That day, he'd almost gotten his hands on April McCree at last. He'd been within a hairbreadth of dealing with Joseph Carrigan. Both situations had gone unresolved.

One more chance remained to redeem the day. At the very least he could deal with the other Carrigan brother—assuming he was still locked in the jail.

A weary Hank Coldwell at last reached the jail. He glanced through the office window and was pleased to find the office momentarily empty. He headed back to the rear of the building and looked cautiously through a cell window.

There was Liam Carrigan, sleeping on his bunk. Coldwell smiled. Then he glanced up and was amazed and delighted to recognize the man in the far cell: Joseph Carrigan! Joseph was not sleeping, but pacing back and forth, looking as restless and eager for freedom as a panther in a cage.

Coldwell couldn't believe his luck. It struck him as hilarious that Joseph Carrigan was now jailed along with his brother. But it wasn't surprising; in fact, he should have anticipated it. The law had probably showed up at their fight in the alley.

If Joseph wanted out of that cell now, he'd want out a lot worse in a few minutes.

He cocked an ear when he heard a tumult across town. The fire in the empty house had been noticed. A minute later, he heard the clang of the firewagon bell.

The time was right. The jail was empty except for the prisoners, and if the jailer was planning to return, Coldwell would bet he wouldn't until he'd gone to see what the furor was across town. By the time it was discovered that the jail was burning as well, the two prisoners in the back would already be baked.

Coldwell spread coal oil around and upon the rear of the building, emptying a little over half the keg. Then he went to the window of Joseph Carrigan's cell, glass panes with metal bars set in place behind them.

He shattered the glass with the half-empty cask. Joseph started and turned; across in the other cell, Liam Carrigan sat up.

"Hello, gentlemen!" Coldwell said. "I hope you are well this evening . . . a little on the cool side, though. But don't worry, it will warm up soon enough."

"Coldwell!" Joseph said. "What the devil . . ."

Coldwell struck a match and lit the coal oil. Flame licked down the wall and across the cell floor.

"Joseph!" Liam yelled, pulling on the bars of his cell. "Dear God, Joseph, beat out the flames!"

Joseph grabbed the blanket off his bunk and began beating at the fire. But the liquid fuel merely clung to the cloth and refused to go out.

Outside, Coldwell, laughing, lit the coal oil he'd spread on the rear of the building. Flames crawled up the walls.

He set the wooden coal oil cask in the flames to ensure that it burned. They'd figure out soon enough that the fire had been set, but there was no reason to make it too easy.

He whistled as he strode across town toward his boardinghouse. He walked in the front door and greeted the elderly landlady.

"What's happening out there, Mr. Murphy?" she asked. "I heard the fire bell."

"There's a house on fire across town, I think," he said. "I think it's a big one."

"Oh, I hate a fire," she said.

"Don't we all, ma'am. Don't we all. Well, good evening to you."

"Good evening, Mr. Murphy."

Joseph Carrigan pounded at the flames with his blanket, fighting panic. Liam still rattled his bars, roaring with fury and frustration, and shouting for the jailer. Where was he? How could a self-respecting town leave prisoners unguarded?

At last Joseph made progress, the flames losing the battle to the flailing and smoking blanket. Liam felt encouraged, then looked to his left and saw fire lick through a crack in the wall.

The rear of the jail was on fire. What Joseph had just extinguished was only part of the blaze.

Joseph slapped out the last flame, stood panting and coughing, then turned.

"Joseph . . ." Liam pointed toward the rear wall.

"Dear Lord," Joseph whispered. "What can we do?"

Liam shook his head. "Nothing. Nothing. Just shout out the window . . . hope somebody hears us."

"Liam, I heard a fire bell already. Maybe they're on their way."

Liam watched the opening in the wall grow a little wider, the flames a little more visible. The heat and smoke inside the jail was beginning to mount.

Liam went to his window, broke out the glass with his fists, and began to shout for help.

Strictly speaking, it was against the rules to leave the jail untended, especially when cells were occupied, but like most rules in the world of Culpepperville, Missouri, law enforcement, it was generally ignored.

The jailer's name was Tom Hilliott. He walked across town with a covered plate of food in his hands, distracted by the action and fury across town. It was a big fire, that much he could tell. Orange light played on the smoke that billowed skyward, and occasionally he could see leaping flames reaching above the skyline.

The old Campbell place, damaged by last year's tornado and abandoned ever since. That was the best he could figure. He'd always thought that place was a fire hazard, and eventually some vagrant or vandal would set it afire either by accident or just to watch the show.

And quite a show it would be! That old place would burn spectacularly . . . and Hilliott enjoyed watching a good fire as much as the next man. Odds were, he could sneak over there, find a good vantage point where he wouldn't be noticed and reported to the marshal for not being on duty. If he could get away with leaving the jail to buy his second supper of the night, he could get away with sneaking off to watch a fire.

He rounded a corner and paused, debating inwardly. Did he dare? The marshal sometimes came by the jail at night, usually on some pretense of needing to pick up something he'd forgotten or just to see how things were moving along, but Hilliott knew the real reason was to check up on him and make sure he was doing what he should.

Hilliott had a feeling that tonight might be one of those nights, or at least it would be if he gave in to the temptation to go watch the fire. Better head back to the jail, at least for now.

He walked another block, turned another corner, and dropped his plate of food right in the street.

The jail had a strange light about it, emanating from the rear. He ran forward and felt his bowels loosen and threaten to empty themselves as he realized the jail was afire. The entire rear of it was flaming . . . the rear section where the two prisoners were.

Hilliott swallowed hard, braced himself, and raced for the front door. He had to get the prisoners out, if he could. If it wasn't too late already.

16

He slammed open the front door and entered the smoke-filled office. Fanning the air, battling smoke, coughing, he went to the corner where the key ring hung on a peg. The keys were gone! He nearly lost the battle with his bowels again, then remembered he'd dropped the keys in the desk drawer. Choking on thick gray smoke, he went to the desk and yanked open the drawer so hard that its contents went flying. The key ring clattered to the floor. He stooped to pick it up, noticed the air was clearer near the floor, and dropped to his hands and knees. He crawled toward the door of the cellblock, reached up, and opened it.

Heat and even thicker smoke struck him. He crawled forward, dragging the keys on the floor.

"Mr. Carrigan! Mr. Jefferson! Are you alive?"

He heard two shouts, weakened by inhaled smoke. Thank God! They were both still alive! He'd rescue them, gain their gratitude, and persuade them not to reveal he'd been out of the jail tonight.

"I'm coming!" he said. "I've got the key!"

"Hurry!" the one he knew as Jefferson shouted. "We're about to give out back here!"

He hurried into the smoke and heat, fumbling clumsily with the key ring. Though the flooring of the cells was a sheet of metal, between the cells it was only wood, and quite rough and worn wood at that, with huge gaps that let up drafts. At the moment those drafts were feeding air to the flames, making them all the hotter.

"Hurry!" Liam urged, hand across his face.

"I'm . . . trying . . ." But Hilliott's hand shook so badly he could hardly function.

Liam dropped to the floor, sucking in cleaner air. While he was down there, he saw the key ring drop from Hilliott's hand, right through a crack in the floor and beneath the jail.

"Oh, no!" Hilliott exclaimed. "Oh, Jesus help me, Jesus help me . . ."

"Go down there and get those keys!" Liam roared. "You got to find them fast!"

"There's an extra key . . . up front somewhere, somewhere . . ."

"Go get it!" Joseph demanded. He was near to collapse, struggling for air.

The jailer ran to the front and out the door.

Liam looked over at Joseph. "Pray he doesn't just panic and run away."

Joseph, hacking badly, nodded. "I'm already praying," he managed to squeak out.

A minute went by. They heard nothing beneath the jail to indicate Hilliott had gotten down there. Maybe he wouldn't even try.

"He's abandoned us," Joseph said. "He's left us to cook like hens in an oven."

At that moment, Liam saw something poke up through the hole that had swallowed the key ring. It was one edge of the ring. It stuck, disappeared, then appeared again, and this time came all the way through.

"He's poked the key ring up from below, Joseph! I can't reach it!"

Joseph dropped to his face, put an arm out through the bars, and slapped around until he got his hand on the key ring. Rising, he began trying the keys until he found one that opened his door.

"Hallelujah!" Liam declared, as Joseph's cell door opened.

Joseph came across and opened Liam's door as well. Together they stumbled, coughing, up to the front office. They paused long enough to kick open the cabinet that held the personal effects of prisoners. Everything inside was theirs. Grabbing their goods, they staggered out the door, across the street, and vanished into an alley. There they coughed and spat and wept and chuckled and cursed and prayed.

"Should we go back and thank that jailer?" Liam asked.

"We should go back and make sure he got out from under the jail all right," Joseph said.

"He did," Liam replied, pointing.

Sure enough, there was Hilliott, standing in front of the jail, silhouetted against it, watching it burn. Others appeared around him.

"Anybody inside?" they heard someone ask the jailer.

"No, no. It's empty."

"That's good."

"Yeah."

"How'd it start?"

"I don't know."

Liam and Joseph knew, but they'd not be sharing information tonight. They'd spent all the time in the jail that they would. Time to get out of their smoky clothes and into something clean. Time to find April McCree . . . if she was still alive to be found.

They moved through alleys and back lots and made their way toward the hotel. At the livery they paused to wash themselves as best they could at the water trough, though the smell of smoke would linger with them for some time.

While they were shaking themselves dry, Liam pointed at the southern skyline. "The jail's not in that direction, but I see fire."

Joseph nodded. "There is a fire. Two things burning in the same town on the same night! Do you think Coldwell set both?"

"I don't know."

"I think maybe he did . . . I think what's burning in that direction may be the old house where his nephew's body was."

"Burning it to hide the body?"

"Maybe so. I don't know. All I know is I'm glad to be alive, and I want to get to the hotel."

"What about April McCree?"

"Maybe she'll be there. She's got a key."

"Or maybe Coldwell's already gotten her."

"I hope not. I despise him, Liam. I intend to see that son of a bitch pay for what he's done. Any man who would kill for money isn't fit to live."

"There wasn't anybody paying him to try to kill us."

"No. He did that entirely on his own. Which makes me all the more determined to get him. Let's go. The hotel is waiting."

"They'll come looking for us there, Joseph. We're escapees, sort of."

"We won't be there to be found. We'll get into some fresh clothes, gather our things, and fetch our horses and tack gear from the stable. Then we'll find a barn or some place to lie low for tonight."

"And after that?"

"We keep looking for April McCree, and if we find her, we help her."

"And if we find Coldwell instead?"

"I say we send him to join his nephew."

"Amen."

They entered the hotel through the window, and realized at once they were not alone.

"I'll kill you!" a quaking female voice said from the darkness. "Don't move another step!"

"April McCree?" Liam said.

"Is it . . ."

"Yes, April. It's us. Joseph and Liam Carrigan."

Joseph struck a match, and they saw her standing there with a pistol raised, gripped in both hands. She lowered it when she saw who they were.

"Thank God it's you," she said. "Thank God!"

Joseph shook out the match.

In the darkness, Liam approached her, hesitated, then put his arms around her.

"It's going to be all right now," he said. "It's going to be all right. We're going to take care of you, and your baby."

She wept. For two minutes they stood there like that in the dark, April weeping in Liam's arms, Joseph standing by the window, watching, saying nothing because there was, at the moment, nothing else that needed saying.

17

It had been a devilishly long and eventful day. As Joseph looked back over it, he found it nearly impossible to believe that it was only the night before he'd been in the little house of Plunker Freeman, sipping coffee and hearing the old man's tale of the unfortunate young fighter, Pat Carrigan, and Freeman's seemingly loco speculation that the fire that had burned the hotel at Hooper was started, directly or indirectly, by none other than the famous Crane Hart Maxwell.

Now Joseph wasn't so inclined to dismiss much of anything as loco. In the course of a single day he'd been battered and bruised in a fall through a damaged staircase, had seen a man killed with a nail through the temple, had very nearly gotten killed himself by an infamous hired gunman, had been arrested, survived a jail fire, and found, lost, then found again a tragic young pregnant woman whom someone apparently wanted dead.

Now Joseph leaned back against the wall of a barn loft that was tonight's residence for himself, his brother, and April McCree. And despite the exhaustion that gripped all of them, there was too much to be told for sleep to be the priority. It was time to find some answers.

"I want to ask you something, April," Joseph said. "Today you told me I reminded you of someone. Is that person Pat Carrigan, the fighter who disappeared over in Hooper?"

She looked at him, her pretty face only dimly visible in the light of the moon coming through the open loft ventilation window. "It is. Your eyes are so much like his . . . your face. When you held up the matches today so I could see your face while you were down in that cellar, you looked so much like him that I thought he had somehow come back to me. But he can't come back . . . he's dead."

"Killed by the same men who have pursued you?"

"Yes."

"Do you know who the men are?"

"I don't know their names."

"The one you killed today with the board and the nail was named Sam Leisure. The other one is named Hank Coldwell. Have you heard that name before?"

She said, "I think I have. I don't know where."

"He's a rather famous fellow," Liam said. "Famous for killing people. He's a hired murderer, and his price, they say, doesn't come cheap."

If they anticipated any reaction from her, she let them down. "I am not surprised. The one who wants me dead can afford any price."

"Who wants you dead, April?" Liam asked.

"You wouldn't believe me if I told you," she said.

"I'd believe you if you told me it was Crane Hart Maxwell," said Joseph.

"Is it true, Miss McCree?"

"Yes," she said. "It's true." She looked away.

"I have another question, and I hope you'll take no offense that I ask it."

"I could hardly take offense at anything said to me by men who have given so much of themselves, even in only one day, to help me."

"Then I'll ask, and beg your pardon if I shouldn't. I was told that the fire that burned the hotel at Hooper started in Maxwell's room the night he was there. I was told that there was a young woman in the room, and that she and Maxwell were heard to be arguing. Miss McCree, was that—"

"I was the woman," she said.

Joseph nodded. "I thought so. It made sense. And now, another question, more prone to offend you, so

I apologize in advance. Is the baby you carry the child of Maxwell?"

She lifted her head a little. "Why do you ask that question?"

"Because, miss, it seems to me that if that's his child, it might explain why he is so determined to see you . . . removed. A man with eyes on the presidency of the nation is hardly helped by having a bastard child . . . forgive me . . . on his personal ledger."

"He is not the father of my child. The father of my child is the man I love . . . loved, Patrick Carrigan."

"Then why is Maxwell so determined to see you dead?"

She rose and paced back and forth before the window, her form a dark and sweeping thing against the vague illumination of the night sky. "There is a saying, or perhaps it's a verse in the Bible . . . your sins will find you out. I can testify in my own life that this is the truth. I've not had an easy life, and I've not done what is right. I was left an orphan child early in my life . . . I did what I had to do to survive."

She stopped, then turned to face them. "I will mince no words. I was the mistress of Crane Maxwell for two years. I remained his mistress even after his marriage. But I didn't love him. I loved Patrick Carrigan. And when I discovered that I carried Patrick's baby, I made the mistake of believing that Crane would let me have my freedom to marry the man I loved." She stopped and reached up to wipe a tear. "I was . . . very wrong. He was infuriated. He told me that I had betrayed him. He vowed to kill Patrick and to keep me as his own possession, no matter what the result for him or his career. He told me he . . . loved me. But it was a lie. The only true love of Crane Hart Maxwell is himself. The only love he has for others is to own and control them and use them."

"He had Patrick killed."

"Yes. Patrick was a fighter by trade . . . he traveled from town to town, fighting at saloons and in back lots and so on. Maxwell hired a man—you tell me now it was this Coldwell—and sent him to find Patrick. And they took him out on the plains . . . and killed him."

"I'm sorry," Liam murmured. Joseph nodded agreement.

She wiped more tears and took a step closer to them. "Do you know how Crane Maxwell told me what he'd done? Can you guess? He brought me on one of his excursions, took me to a tiny town called Hooper. I couldn't understand quite why he'd want to spend the night at so small a place, where there was no crowd to be drawn. But he'd taken me there so he could tell me what he'd done to Patrick . . . tell me at the very place he'd had him killed." She bowed her head and put her hands on her face. "Oh, God! Oh, God!"

Joseph rose and clumsily made his way to her. He put an arm around her as Liam watched—a reversal of the situation earlier in the hotel room. Joseph glanced over at Liam and made out a dim view of his face, looking at him somberly, then looking away.

"That was why we raised our voices in that hotel. I couldn't believe, wouldn't believe, what he told me. I couldn't accept that anyone could be so cruel, and that Patrick had been killed. I angered him . . . he slapped me. A lamp was knocked over. The hotel burned, but I escaped. I suppose he couldn't bear that I had gotten away from him. So now he's sent his killers after me as well. To kill me, and to kill the baby that is all that remains of the man who got from me the one thing I would not give Crane Maxwell."

"Your love," Joseph said.

"Yes." She looked up at him, her face inches from his. "You are so like Patrick. So similar!"

Liam coughed loudly and scuffed his feet on the loft floor.

Joseph took his arm from around her and moved away, reluctantly.

"Tell us about Patrick's family," Liam said.

"He didn't talk about them much. His mother died giving him birth. He and his father had fought over something or another in the past. They were estranged."

"Was his father's name also Patrick?"

"Yes. Pat's father was born in Ireland and came to this nation years ago."

"Did Pat ever mention an uncle?"

"Yes. Still in Ireland, to Pat's knowledge."

"No," Joseph said. "He came to America, like his older brother. He lived in Nashville, Tennessee, and raised two sons."

She smiled. "No wonder I see so much of him in your face. You are his cousin."

"What about me?" Liam said. "I'm as much a cousin as Joseph is."

"You are like him, too. But I think Joseph is a little more."

Liam stood and walked to the window. "I need a cigar. And I'm clean out."

"We'll get some more tomorrow. But now the question is, what do we do? Where do we go? We've still got a hired killer out there who wants April dead."

"There is a place I can go," she said. "I have an uncle, in the mountains of Colorado. He lives in a remote place. I think I would be safe there . . . safe to have my and Patrick's baby."

"Colorado," Liam said. "That's a hell of a trip for a woman in your condition."

"Better that than to stay here and be tracked down by Hank Coldwell."

"May I ask you both something?" she said.

"Of course," Joseph replied.

"Why do you smell so of smoke?"

"Well," Joseph said, "we had a run-in ourselves with Coldwell. He tried to burn down the jail with us in it."

"I didn't know."

"As you can see, he didn't succeed, though he very nearly did."

"He's not only your enemy now. He's ours, too."

"I hate him," she said.

"I'm not very fond of him, either," Liam replied.

In the dark boardinghouse, Hank Coldwell opened his eyes wide, then sat up.

"No!" he whispered. "Oh, no . . . not now!"

He got out of bed and stood, hand on the bedpost, breath coming hard. "No!" he said again.

On the bedside table was a hairbrush. He picked it up and clamped it between his teeth, barely before the seizure hit. It threw him back onto the bed, where every muscle stiffened and his entire body quaked violently. He bit hard into the handle of the hairbrush, his teeth cutting into the wood.

How long it went on he couldn't tell. His next consciousness was of being on the floor, seated, leaning back against the side of the bed. He removed the hairbrush from his mouth and looked at it. He'd left clear and deep impressions of his teeth in the wood.

The old woman was at the door, knocking gently. "Mr. Murphy? Are you all right?"

He wanted to curse her and tell her to go away, but he restrained himself. "I'm fine . . . I just fell. But I'm fine."

"Are you sure?"

"Of course I'm sure."

"Good night, then, Mr. Murphy."

He listened to her shuffle away. For five minutes he remained where he was, then got into bed again and pulled the covers up around his shoulders.

18

Joseph leaned on the fence at the horse trader's lot and kept his head lowered and hat pulled down a little farther on his brow than usual. He sought to look as relaxed as possible, but his eyes scanned constantly all around him, looking for Coldwell. He was eager to get this transaction done, rejoin Liam and April, and get out of this town.

The horse trader had a clubfoot and moved slowly. He limped out of his office, across the lot, and handed Joseph a stack of bills. "There you are, Mr. Smith. Count it if you wish, but it's all there."

Joseph pocketed the money. "I trust you completely, sir. Thank you."

They shook hands. "You have the smell of smoke on you, sir," the trader said. "Were you at one of the fires last night?"

"I watched the old house burn down. I hear there was a jail fire as well."

"That's true. A couple of prisoners almost got themselves cooked, but the jailer freed them at great risk to his own life. I've got a friend who runs a little twice-a-month newspaper here, and he's going to write up a story about him as a hero. Of course, the prisoners got away once he let them out, but it doesn't matter. They were due to be freed anyway, as I hear the story."

"Anybody know how the fires started?"

"Nobody's figured out the one at the jail. Me, I figure the prisoners did it themselves. Foolish, but people do things like that. As for the house, I think there was a body inside it. Way too burned up to recognize. It was probably a vagrant who started up a fire to keep warm, and it got away from him."

"Sad."

"Yes. Liquor makes a man into a wretched creature, unable to take care of himself."

"Amen. I seldom touch the stuff, myself. Well, it's been a pleasure doing business with you, sir."

"Same to you, Mr. Smith."

An hour later, Liam Carrigan stood in the semi-darkness of a musty boxcar, peering out around the edge of the nearly closed sliding door. "I think we're in the clear," he said. "The railroad man is aboard now. Looks like these stowaways have managed to get away with it."

He slid the door closed and turned toward Joseph and April, who were seated amid casks and crates. Seated a little too close to one another, it seemed to Liam, and he didn't like it. "I still say it would have been easier to buy a ticket and ride this train as passengers instead of illegal freight," he said.

Neither Joseph nor April answered. They'd already talked through that matter in advance. April was persuaded that to ride as an open passenger would draw attention and create a trail by which she might be tracked. And certainly it was true that someone as ragged and dirty as she would draw attention on a passenger train.

So they'd come up with an alternative plan in the barn loft. Sell the horses, board a boxcar, and get out of Missouri as quickly and secretly as possible. Break the trail so that Coldwell could not easily follow it. If they were lucky, they'd make it all the way to Colorado without being caught. Once there, they'd take up the matter of how best to find their way to the remote home of April's mountain-dwelling uncle.

Joseph reached over and took April's hand, holding it tenderly. Liam watched from the corner of his eye, swore silently to himself, and began pacing as the train jolted and began to move.

"There's something we need to do for you as quickly as we can," he said. "We need to get you to a doctor and make sure that all you've been through hasn't endangered your child."

"I think I'm fine. But I'd do that . . . I want my baby to be healthy and strong, like his father was. Or maybe her father."

"It will be hard, raising a child alone."

"Yes. But I'll do it. And I believe I'll do it well."

"I believe you will, too."

Liam pulled out a partly smoked cigar and relit it, muttering to himself while he did so. Joseph looked over at him. "Be careful with that, Liam. There's some loose straw in this car, and you could set it ablaze."

"Do tell, Grandma! I'll be careful. Maybe you should tell me if I need to button my shirt different, too."

"Beg pardon, Liam. It seems you're touchy this morning." Joseph winked at April, but she didn't notice it.

"Joseph, why don't you go find your own boxcar to ride in and leave a man in peace."

"What the devil's wrong with you?"

"What do you think? We've got a hired killer after an innocent woman, and after us, too, and you sit there smiling and jovial like an old maid at a tea party! You annoy the very . . . the very stuffing out of me sometimes, Joseph. Beg pardon, ma'am."

"What do you want me to do? Get up and pace

and smoke a cigar? I guess I should do that. That really makes all the difference in a situation like this."

"Joseph, just shut up."

Joseph smiled at April. "A wielder of a devastatingly sharp wit, my brother is."

She withdrew her hand from Joseph's and found something to study in the far corner of the boxcar. Joseph lost his smile, and Liam gained one.

"Never mind him, April," he said. "Joseph thinks every woman he meets is just waiting to hold his hand."

"I don't think you're in much of a position to criticize anyone else regarding the gentlemanly way to treat a woman. The women you consort with are no more than common harlots."

April came to her feet. "For God's sake, is this the way it's going to be with both of you? Why are you talking this way to each other?"

Both brothers held silent, staring at her in surprise. She turned to Joseph.

"You talk about 'common harlots' in a way that makes them sound like no more than rubbish! Do you not know that there are plenty of people who would look at me and call me a 'common harlot'?"

Joseph stammered, managing to make only noise. Liam stifled a chuckle.

She turned her cannons on him. "And why are you complaining and throwing insults at your own brother when both of you came within minutes of losing each other forever only last night?"

Liam frowned and looked away.

"I'm sorry to be speaking so harshly to you," she said to both of them in a slightly milder tone. "I'm grateful for your help, and I believe God Himself has sent me the very cousins of my lost Patrick to aid me at a time I need it, and I'm so glad that has happened . . . but you must understand that you are both still strangers to me, and right now I'm very tired and very scared. There is a very powerful man who wants me dead, and I'm afraid he'll not stop until he finds me and kills me . . . and my baby. So please pardon me if I have little patience for all this . . . this nonsense, this banter and insult-trading. I'm sorry." She sat down again, looking away from both of them. "I'm sorry," she repeated, much more softly. "I'm so grateful to both of you. I truly am."

A long silence held. At length Liam cleared his throat. "Miss McCree . . . April . . . you have my apology." He paused, then added, "You're right. My brother can be very annoying."

He went to the door of the boxcar, slid it open a few inches, and stood watching the landscape roll by as he puffed on his cigar.

An hour of silent riding brought calm to the occupants of the boxcar. Liam took a brief nap, and

Joseph leaned back against a crate and lost himself in his own thoughts. April toyed with a bit of straw and seemed preoccupied.

She broke the silence at last. "Joseph, I think I've heard your name before. But I don't know that it was you being spoken of, or just someone with the same name."

"Who was doing the speaking?"

"Patrick. He told me that he'd read something in a newspaper about a deputy in Dodge City who apparently overcame an entire gang of thieves, single-handedly. Patrick noticed it because the deputy had the same last name as him. Was it you?"

Joseph looked uncomfortable with the question. Liam, leaning back and resting, spoke from beneath the hat tilted down across his face. "Yes, it was Joseph."

"It wasn't an entire gang of thieves. Just a few men who'd broken into a freight office."

"It was an entire gang of thieves," Liam said.

"That's very remarkable. You are obviously a very capable man."

"It was as much good fortune and circumstances as anything else," Joseph said.

Liam sat up. "Don't let him fool you, April. What he did was very outstanding. I was proud of him then and am proud of him now. But he's not prone to talk much about it."

"Well . . . it makes me feel safer to know I'm in the company of heroic men."

"One, at least," Liam said. "When I was in Dodge the best thing I did was help repair a few wagons. My brother was getting his name in the papers as a famous gun-toting lawman, and I was hammering the rims on wagon wheels."

"I know already of your heroism, Liam," she said, smiling. "I saw it the night I hid in your room."

"Why did you leave? When I came back and found you gone, it crossed my mind that maybe Coldwell had gotten you. Of course, I didn't know he was Coldwell at the time."

"I would guess that when you saw I'd taken your money, other things may have crossed your mind, too."

"I admit that I did briefly consider the possibility that the entire thing had been a ploy to get that money. But I gave up that idea right away because the pieces didn't really fit."

"I left the room because I was afraid to stay. When Coldwell came to the door I knew that he'd tracked me down, and I couldn't bear to stay anyplace where he knew I was. Then I saw the money on the bedside table and took it. I had to do it. I didn't want to."

"Anybody would have done the same in your circumstances. Where did you go?"

"I found a little arbor behind a house and hid there. Then, when morning came, I searched out that empty house and hid there until you found me . . . and *they* found me, too."

"I admire the way you defended yourself against Sam Leisure. You dealt with him very effectively."

"All I did was hit him. I didn't even realize that nail was in the board."

"It did the job."

"Please. I don't take pleasure in any of that. I don't like to talk about such things."

Liam said, "Then let me ask you about something else. How is this uncle of yours going to react to two strangers bringing his niece to him . . . and you being in, uh, a family kind of way?"

"He's a good man. He'll take me in."

"How long since you've had contact with him?"

"A few years."

"Are you sure you'll be able to find his place?"

"I've never been there, but I know the town it is near. Someone will be able to tell us how to get there."

"I hate to ask such a question, but if this uncle is as good a man as that, why didn't he help you out when you were orphaned as a child?"

"He couldn't. He was in jail at that time. I come from a family that doesn't have many smooth edges. By the time he was free and I could have asked him for help, I'd already made so many bad choices that there was not much point in trying to mend my ways. That's how it seemed to me at the time, anyway."

"Well, if he can be found, we'll find him."

"I wish we could have met Patrick," Joseph said. "I'd like to have known him. My own cousin. Liam and I never even knew we had one. Did Patrick have brothers or sisters?"

"No. Just him and his father, alone. But as I told you, they were at odds with each other. It's too bad that they parted without having mended their fences. I doubt Patrick senior even knows that Pat is dead. There's no way he could know."

"Then I guess, when we find him, we'll be the bearers of bad news. I just wish it hadn't happened that way. For Pat."

"God knows I wish it hadn't, too," she said. "God knows."

"Tell us about him," Joseph said.

She smiled sadly. "He was such a good man. A fighter, and tough as a knotted rope, but also kind and gentle. He had a temper, but even so, a great compassion for people. Did you know that at times, he felt sorry for the very men he would defeat in his fights? He told me once that he could tell how embarrassed some of them were, and he felt bad for them."

"Remarkable. How did you meet him?"

She stared at her feet and did not reply for a few moments. "I've not lived a holy life. You know that. I've had poverty and many bad turns of fortune. I've been forced to do things that are not right. Not chaste."

Joseph wondered if he was about to hear that she had met Pat in an arrangement of prostitution.

"There was a man once. Outside St. Louis. He became interested in me because he'd learned, or at least been able to reasonably guess, that I was keeping company with Crane Maxwell. He thought that stealing the 'possession' of such a famous man would give him some sort of badge of merit, I suppose. He tried to force himself on me.

"Pat was there. He'd actually been brought in for Maxwell's entertainment, fighting a couple of Maxwell's bodyguards in a sort of exhibition. He won, of course. He almost always won. In any case, when the fighting was through, he came upon the man I mentioned, and me. The man had dragged me off and was doing his best to have his way with me. I was struggling and resisting. Patrick stepped in. Two quick blows from those big fists of his, and the man was out cold. It was astonishing to see how expertly he did it."

"And that was the start between you and him."

"Yes. I'd never met anyone like him. I've not met anyone like him since."

Liam scuffed his foot and made a little coughing sound in his throat after she said that. Joseph recognized the sound. Liam made that noise sometimes when he was disappointed and trying to cover it.

"Pat didn't care that I was under the thumb of Maxwell," April said. "We started finding ways to see one another. He began following Maxwell's travel route, doing his exhibition fights along the way to make money and trying not to draw Maxwell's attention. He did that for me . . . I didn't want Maxwell's attention drawn to the fact I was seeing someone else. I knew how dangerous it would be for Pat. He didn't fully appreciate that. He wasn't afraid of anyone or anything. If it had been up to him, I think he'd have marched up to Maxwell himself and told him he was taking me away. But I wouldn't let him."

She paused. "I should never have let Pat stay around me. I should have known that Maxwell would find out what was going on. For Pat's sake I should have just broken it all off with him. He'd not have been killed."

"You have the same right to love somebody as anybody else does, the way I see it," Liam said.

"I know. But when your loving somebody gets him killed, what good is it? What is that except just a sorrow and a grief that you can never hope to get past?"

She drew in a deep, ragged breath, her eyes reddening. "I don't think I want to talk anymore," she said.

Hank Coldwell typically did not sleep late, but today was an exception. His exhausting activity of the prior day, combined with the nocturnal seizure that very exhaustion helped prompt, had left him drained. He slept through the landlady's breakfast, and by the time he rose, washed himself at the basin, and left the boardinghouse, the sun was halfway across the eastern half of the sky.

Despite the difficult night, Coldwell felt relatively lively. There was still the girl to be found and eliminated, but he at least had the satisfaction of having roasted the Carrigan brothers.

Coldwell stopped in a bakery and purchased a small loaf of sweet bread as a late breakfast. He nibbled it and strode through a town still heavy with the smoke of two fires. The stench actually gave him pleasure.

He worked his way around to the area of the jail and relished the sight of the flattened, smoking, black structure. The cells remained, but they were twisted and distorted. Wonderful, blistering heat, enough to misshape metal . . . what must it have done to the bodies of the two brothers?

He stood chewing his bread, watching the smoke rise from the rubble, when a man walked up beside him.

"Two fires in one night . . . hell of a thing, huh?"

"Nothing you'd expect," Coldwell replied.

"I saw both fires. The empty house burned bigger and brighter, but I swear, I think this jail burned hotter. You couldn't even get close to it. Amazing that anybody got out alive."

Coldwell stopped chewing. "What?"

"Got out. The prisoners. Amazing they got out alive."

"How the hell . . ."

"The jailer sprang them. Good of him to do that. Nobody except the worst murderer would deserve to die locked up in a box. Nobody but the worst murderer. I say, in a situation like that, let 'em out and let 'em go."

"I'll be damned," Coldwell said. He tossed the bread to the ground. "I'll be damned . . . they got away!"

"It is amazing, ain't it! Something wrong with that bread?"

"I'm not hungry."

"Whoever was in the house, he wasn't so fortunate. He sure didn't get away. Nothing left of him much but a few bones, some teeth, and a belt buckle."

"Belt buckle . . ."

"That's what I hear. Well, see you around, friend."

Coldwell stood there staring at nothing. Belt buckle. He should have remembered. Sam's belt buckle, made of heavy, hard metal . . . his name engraved on the back of it.

Dear Lord, they'd be able to identify Sam by that belt buckle. And among those who knew such things, the name Sam Leisure was associated with that of Hank Coldwell.

The day suddenly seemed dark. He turned and walked numbly back toward his boardinghouse.

He hated this town. It had cost him his only real friend, his nephew, his partner . . . and all of those he had set out to destroy remained alive.

And by now, they were probably gone. Gone God only knew where . . . and how he'd track them again, he couldn't suppose.

He reached the boardinghouse and the old woman was there, standing in the doorway. "A telegram has come for you, Mr. Murphy." She handed it to him.

He read it, then read it again.

"Mr. Murphy, you look pale. Are you well?"

He wadded up the telegram and thrust it into a pocket.

"I'll be leaving, right away," he said.

"So soon?"

"Yes."

"I hope the hospitality hasn't been bad, Mr. Murphy."

"Your hospitality has been fine. But I have to go. Today."

He entered the house and began packing his possessions.

19

When Crane Hart Maxwell put aside state politics and turned his full attention to private enterprise and national aspirations, he established his headquarters in Denver, on the upper floor of a solidly built stone building that looked like a bank but which in fact had been built for no other purpose than being a worthy living monument to the great Maxwell. Through the doors of that stone edifice had passed presidents, congressmen, senators, writers of note, actors, famous clergymen, and international dignitaries. To be called to Maxwell Hall, as the building became known, was to be honored, set apart, validated, and vindicated.

But Maxwell was a man who reveled in the defying of expectations and the rejection of the obvious. Four years after his move to Denver he surprised a nation when he announced that he would vacate Maxwell Hall and leave the city of Denver altogether, taking up residence instead in a small Rocky Mountain mining town that had been built around a small, short-lived strike. When the color began to run out, Crane Hart Maxwell came in, buying out the entire town, building himself a mansion surrounded by spectacular gardens, moving in his staff, his associates, and creating and sustaining an entire town's commerce. Houses were built, sold, and occupied. Merchants opened stores in a place where no store should succeed, and thrived. Maxwell himself saw to it, when necessary, but at length the town of Maxwell began to be self-sustaining. Visitors swarmed to it, ogling Maxwell's huge mansion and expansive gardens and spending their money in the stores and shops he'd helped set up and initially subsidized. A smart railroad entrepreneur gained Maxwell's support in building a spur line to the town, and others of the nation's elite and wealthy began moving into the vicinity, heightening their own splendor by catching the reflected greater splendor of Maxwell himself.

His offices were in an edifice much like that he'd vacated in Denver, albeit smaller, a sort of junior version of Maxwell Hall. He held court behind two huge oak doors with gleaming brass fittings.

Outside that doorway, two days after he left Culpepperville, Missouri, Hank Coldwell sat smoking an expensive cigar and trying to look much more relaxed than he really was.

The telegram that had drawn him there remained

in his pocket, uncrumpled now and neatly folded. He didn't need to keep the message . . . but a man simply didn't throw away a communication from the private telegraph line of Crane Hart Maxwell. It simply wasn't done.

Charles Halforth, personal assistant to the Great One himself, sat at a broad desk in front of the big doorways. The smell of Coldwell's cigar offended him, and Coldwell knew it. It was half or more of the reason he was smoking the thing.

A bell on the wall chimed softly. Halforth stood.

"Mr. Coldwell, you may now enter," he said. "You will, however, extinguish the cigar."

"Certainly." Coldwell crushed it out in the marble ashtray on a silver stand beside his chair. He stood slowly, a deliberate move designed to show that the famed Hank Coldwell hurried for no one, not even Maxwell.

He walked around Halforth's desk. The doors opened, seemingly of their own accord, though Coldwell knew that Halforth had triggered some hidden mechanism. Halforth waved him in. He entered, and the doors closed behind him.

Crane Hart Maxwell sat at a desk so huge that it dwarfed Halforth's. He didn't look up as Coldwell advanced. Coldwell stopped three feet in front of the desk and stood, looking at his employer with an expression of forced unconcern.

Maxwell, studying an official-looking document of some sort, continued to ignore Coldwell. At length Coldwell cleared his throat, and said, "I'm here."

Maxwell's gray eyes lifted slowly and studied Coldwell with near contempt. He slowly lowered his papers to the gleaming desktop.

"I was under the impression, Mr. Coldwell, that you are a man who did not fail at the tasks he is assigned."

"I don't fail."

"Then I can assume that April McCree is dead?"

"No, sir. Not yet. She will be."

"You know where she is, then."

A pause. "Not precisely."

"Not at all, you mean."

"Not at the moment, no."

"But you did kill Patrick Carrigan."

"I fired the shot myself."

"You should have fired another. He's not dead."

Coldwell could only stare. His mouth went dry. "I beg your pardon?"

"He's been seen, Mr. Coldwell. Left arm in a sling, a bandage on his shoulder. But very much alive."

"I shot him through the heart!"

"No. You shot him through the shoulder. And obviously you decided there was no need for a coup de grace."

Coldwell frowned. "There's got to be a mistake. He has to be dead."

"You shot him, you assumed you'd killed him, and you rode away."

"I rode away because I knew he was dead."

"He was not dead, and is not dead. And he's somewhere in this vicinity. No doubt thinking that his lovely April will be brought here, and perhaps he can reclaim her."

"If she's brought here, Mr. Maxwell, it will be in a box."

"I'm beginning to think that won't happen, sir. Not until I find someone of greater capabilities than you."

"You'll not find anyone of greater capabilities."

"Where is your partner?"

Hesitation. "Dead."

"How?"

"Killed by someone who was protecting the girl. As best I can tell, that's what happened."

"Who?"

"A fellow name of Joseph Carrigan."

"Carrigan."

"That's right."

"A relation of the unslayable Patrick?"

"I don't know. I figure he probably is."

"Where is he now?"

"I don't know. He's got a brother, a tall bastard

name of Liam. I figure the pair of them have spirited off the girl. But I'll find her."

"How will you do that?"

Coldwell had no answer.

Maxwell stood, and walked around the desk. "I'll tell you something, sir. You'll not find her. You lack the skills and the resources. It may be that no one, not even I, will be able to find her. Because you've failed, she may go into such deep hiding that she becomes unfindable."

"So what do you want from me? If you're not happy with my work, then we end our relationship. Your loss if you do. You'll find no one better than me at what I do."

"You know, Mr. Coldwell, it's unbecoming to see a man trying to strut while he's standing still . . . with his knees trembling at that. I notice such things. Your bravado does nothing to disguise a fact we both know: This affair has not gone as it should have."

Coldwell said nothing; he just stood there, trying to look as haughty as possible.

"Do you know why I've called you back here?"

"I figure you aim to fire me."

"Surprisingly, I'm not going to do that. I'm a man of fairness, even mercy of a sort, Mr. Coldwell. I'm going to give you a second chance. I think I know where she can be found."

Coldwell lifted one brow.

"Have you ever heard of Brasstown?"

"Mining town, I think. Somewhere here in Colorado."

"That's right. And about ten miles above it, there's another settlement . . . not even really a settlement, just a tiny mining camp. It's called Chess. And April McCree has an uncle who lives there. Her only living relative. She actually told me about him herself . . . had a rather romanticized view of him and his life, it seemed to me. He's nothing but a poor miner, a hermit, really. But she seemed to view him as some sort of lonely king of the mountains, living a life of splendid solitude. Someday, she used to tell me, she'd live a life of solitude, and enjoy it. That's where she is, sir. I'd bet on it . . . I *am* betting on it, and despite your failure, also on you. I'm giving you another chance."

"You want me to go after her in this little place her uncle is?"

"Why, maybe you do have some intelligence about you after all. You catch on very quickly!"

"Do you know that she'll be there?"

"I do not. But I'm willing to gamble that she is. It's the natural place she would go to hide."

"I'll need some help. Those two brothers will be with her. They're harder to kill than empty ticks . . . and now, because of them, I've got no partner to help me."

"I agree that you need help. You've already proven your inabilities to me. And I've got you help. Four men, all hard-as-stone hearts and ready to do whatever I tell them. I'm sending them with you."

"Who are they?"

"Pete Wayne. Killed six men in a single fight over in Indiana. One of the best pistoleers in the nation. Kirby Boone, old pistol fighter out of Missouri. Rode with a rebel renegade band and helped shoot up quite a few towns. Rodney Elton, hired gunman who uses a shotgun with sawed-off barrels more often than not. Bad eyes, they say, so he likes a weapon that cuts a wide swath. And last, Pap Grimmer, an old Kentucky fellow who made a name for himself after the war, doing killings for revenge whenever and wherever. No conscience whatsoever, and no mercy. That will be your group."

"My group, you say. So they'll answer to me?"

"For the moment. If you fail again, though, it will be me they'll be expected to listen to. And I'll tell them to bring your carcass in so I can finish you myself."

"You'd not get the chance. I'll leave all four of them for crow bait before I'd let that happen."

"You're cocksure for someone who just let a twenty-three-year-old pregnant woman make a fool of him."

Coldwell presented an icy smile. "If I'm cocksure,

I'll tell you why. You're standing there downtalking me, threatening me, telling me what a failure I am . . . and in the same breath you're putting me in charge of a band of gunmen good enough that I've actually heard of every one of them. And you wouldn't do that if you didn't know I was, in fact, the best. And that's why I'm cocksure, Mr. Maxwell."

Maxwell leaned back against his desk. "Let me talk very directly to you, Coldwell. I'm not a man who abides failure for long, nor defiance. I'm a man with a destiny and a man who must, *must*, be served by a great machine that functions as it should. Gravel in the gearwork, whether it be young women who betray me and get themselves impregnated by their outside lovers, or hired gunmen who can't seem to find their way in either the day or the dark, simply can't be allowed to go on. I shall one day occupy the premiere post in this nation, sir. I cannot afford mistakes or ineptitude." He put forward a long finger and tapped it on Coldwell's chest. "I am giving you one more chance because you cannot have earned the reputation you have without some merit to back it up. You have one more chance to display that merit to me. I want April McCree dead. And this lover of hers, the one you've already failed once to kill."

"Whoever has been seen around here cannot be Patrick Carrigan," Coldwell said flatly. "I shot him through the heart. He is dead."

"No, sir. He is not. Now, get away from here. I've interrupted my great swing across the nation in order to come back here and meet with you. I'll remain here until the successful completion of your venture. Now, leave me. Halforth will take you to meet your new partners."

"My underlings. Not partners. I worked with only one partner, and he's gone."

"And the loss is not a great one, not in my judgment. Now go. I have much work to do and have wasted enough time already."

"Let me help you up there, April."

"No thank you, Liam," she said, swinging up onto the mule without difficulty. She was clad now in the clothing of a man, items bought at a trading post over in Brasstown. Canvas pants, a heavy shirt, rugged blue coat, a hat with a crown big enough to accommodate her hair, heavy miner's boots. Liam wouldn't have thought that a woman dressed so could possibly still look feminine, but April McCree was managing to do so. She perched atop the old mule, newly purchased by Joseph after much haggling, and smiled at Liam. "I've ridden mules before," she said. "When I was a little girl, visiting my uncle Michael. He had two mules, big and gentle as they could be, and he let me ride them, just for fun. It's one of the best memories I have from my childhood . . . and I don't have many. So I like mules."

Joseph came from behind a tree, giving a final hitch to the fly of his trousers. He was a modest fellow by nature and two days ago would not have been so casual in the presence of a woman, but two days of travel in the company of April McCree had relaxed him a bit. And he was in a good humor at the moment, relaxing him further. They'd made it this far without incident, traveling almost entirely by railroad, and inquiries at trading posts and miners' cabins had confirmed for them that Michael McCree indeed remained in these mountains, living near the now-abandoned mining camp called Chess. The last holdout, folks said. Stubbornly clinging to his solitary little kingdom, and now with the town all to himself.

"I have a good name for that mule," Joseph said. "I think we should call him Liam."

"Tell you what," Liam said. "Let's call the front end Liam and the back end Joseph."

"His name is Ben," April said.

"Why Ben?"

"Because he looks like a Ben. Now let's get the packs strapped on around me. I'm eager to get started."

Joseph and Liam worked, placing their few supplies onto the mule in front of and behind April.

"Let me see how he does," she said, when they were finished. She nudged at the mule with her heels and shook the bridle. Rather to the surprise of them all, he began plodding along without any balking. April laughed and began walking him about the meadow, getting used to him.

"Quite a laugh she has, Joseph," Liam said. "Not that she laughs much."

"She's not got much to laugh about, I guess," Joseph replied. "That's a woman in deep grief. Our cousin must have been quite a fellow, to have her love him so much."

"You know, Joseph, we're both in love with her. We may as well admit it."

Joseph nodded. "I know. I can't deny it. But there's no point for either of us, I don't think. Her heart still belongs to a man who is probably lying in some shallow grave out on the plains of Missouri."

"I'd give him back to her if I could, just to make her happy."

"It's the only thing that could make her happy. Except, maybe, bearing his baby. That will be the closest she can come to getting him back again."

They watched her circling Ben the mule in the meadow a few moments more. "Guess we should get started," Liam said. "Lord, I hate to hike! I'd give my eyeteeth for a good mountain horse right now!"

"You can fight with April for rights to ride Ben," Joseph said.

"I've got my pride, Joseph. I'll walk. Come on. Let's go find Michael McCree."

20

Despite the prevailing belief that the healthful bath should be tepid, Crane Hart Maxwell preferred his baths steaming hot. He took them thrice weekly, plus additional ones on special nights. This was a special night.

The tub was nearly full, only a few more bucket-loads of hot water to be brought in by Doolah, his usually unspeaking servant for the past decade. Maxwell, clad in a heavy blue robe, watched the final filling, then stepped to the tub, let Doolah take his robe, and settled carefully into the wonderfully warm water.

Doolah fetched a cigar, clipped its end, and held it down to Maxwell, who clamped his lips around it. Doolah struck a long match and held it while Maxwell puffed the cigar to full light.

"Very good, Doolah. Now, please, tell Halforth to come in here. I've got an errand for him."

Doolah nodded and left the room, leaving Maxwell to soak in luxury.

Halforth, fetched from his own much smaller quarters elsewhere in the building, entered the room ten minutes later.

"Sir."

"Charles, make a run into town for me, please. I'd like Rose's company this evening."

"Yes, sir. Should I instruct her in how she should dress?"

"Tell her to surprise me."

"Yes, sir. I'll not be long in returning."

Within ten minutes, Halforth left the long driveway of the Maxwell edifice. At the closed gate he climbed down, opened the gate, drove the carriage through, then disembarked long enough to lock the gate again. Formerly there had been a guard on hand to do this task, but a bad heart had claimed his life two days earlier, and no replacement had yet been hired.

Halforth proceeded down a winding mountain road into town, stopped at a brick building with little to distinguish it, and entered. A few minutes later, he emerged again, accompanied by a woman of quite elegant appearance, dressed in finery worthy of a ballroom. Halforth helped her into the carriage, then climbed onto the driver's seat.

They set off.

"What was that?" the woman asked.

"What was what, Rose?"

"There was a bumping at the back of the carriage."

"I didn't hear anything."

She shrugged. The carriage rolled on. Reaching the closed gate at Maxwell's place, Halforth again climbed down, opened the gate, and drove through. He stopped the carriage just inside.

He was climbing down from the left side of the driver's perch when a man quietly dropped from the back of the carriage and hurried behind a shrub just inside the gate. The woman, primping at her hair, did not see him.

Halforth closed the gate and climbed back onto the carriage. It rolled forward, up the curving drive.

Maxwell, in his robe again, stood alone before a large mirror, combing his hair quite carefully. He turned his head from side to side, examining a somewhat pockmarked face that in his own perception was perfect. He smiled at his own reflection. A fine evening lay ahead. His wife was absent, as was often the case, off on her own social agenda several states away.

Speaking to the mirror, he said, "Crane, old fellow, you're going to have to learn to do without this kind of thing. You must be discreet . . . it's the discreet man who wins the prize."

But discretion was not in the plans for that night. Later. That night he would worry about nothing, simply enjoy himself in the company of Rose.

He heard her knock and went to the door. Doolah had been dismissed; Crane was alone.

He smiled at her in the doorway. "Ravishing, my dear, as always. Very splendid indeed."

She stepped inside, and he closed the door behind her.

Halforth could reach his own quarters without leaving the building, but it was shorter to exit via a small rear door and cut across the backyard. He was halfway across the yard when movement in the area of the maze of hedges attracted his eye, and his suspicion.

No one should be within the walls. He looked, peering through the darkness. "Doolah?"

Receiving no answer, he reached beneath his coat and drew out a small revolver. He advanced toward the maze.

"Who's there?"

No one answered him. He entered the maze and looked around. Listened, too. Nothing.

His imagination, perhaps. Or a squirrel. Nothing to be concerned over, most likely.

Halforth put away his pistol, walked on across the yard. Along the way, he dropped a small knife that rode in a sheath on the strap of his shoulder holster. He'd dislodged it while handling the pistol. It fell beside his advancing feet and was left behind on the ground as he passed through a decorative grove of aspen trees.

Halforth entered the edifice by another small back door. Within minutes he was undressed, in his bed, and sleeping soundly.

An hour later, Rose, nestling her head on Maxwell's shoulder, reached up to rub playfully at the side of his nose.

"What's the matter, dear?" she asked. "You seem distracted."

"I'm fine."

"Are you not happy yet? Would you like me to pay a little more attention to you, hmmm?" She kissed him softly on the cheek.

"Dammit, woman, it's not that! That kind of thing we've taken care of quite nicely. I'd like some peace now."

She looked hurt and pulled away. "Peace?"

"Yes. I'd like you to leave, Rose. I've got something on my mind."

"What did I do?"

"Nothing. It's not you . . . it's a venture that I've got under way. A job I'm having done. I'm concerned that it may not be done properly."

"Tell me about it."

"No. It's of no concern to you. Listen, just go on to one of the guest chambers and spend the night. Halforth is probably asleep by now, and I'll not disturb him again. Just be sure you are discreet about your presence. Halforth or Doolah can drive you back down come morning."

"Can't I stay here with you?"

"No. Go on. I need some time to think."

She left him there, giving him his time to think, but he found it did him no good. He paced back and forth, feeling ever more unsettled and burdened. "I shouldn't have used Coldwell at all," he muttered to himself. "I should have found myself a different man altogether. I'm not in the slightest bit confident he can do the job."

Too late now. Coldwell and his four new partners were already gone, having left that afternoon to begin the journey toward the remote mountain mining camp of Chess.

Maxwell smoked another cigar, pacing in the large room, then swore aloud, dressed, and left the house. A walk around the grounds would clear his head. Perhaps it was not too late. Perhaps he could send someone after Coldwell and his gang, have Coldwell returned to him . . . and quietly gotten out of the way.

On the other hand, he believed it very likely that April McCree would go to her uncle for refuge at a time such as this. God knows it was the only lead he possessed. If she'd taken off to somewhere else, she might never be found. Or, even worse, be found a year or two after he held the presidency, emerging from the past with her bastard child in tow. She'd said the child was fathered by Patrick Carrigan, the lover with whom she'd betrayed Maxwell. But Maxwell wasn't sure. It might be his child. Heaven forbid, it might look like him! It could ruin him, bring him down.

He paced about in his huge yard, wearing his robe again and wishing he'd put on something heavier. The wind was getting cold that evening. Winter coming on.

Maxwell passed through a small cultivated grove of aspens when a man emerged from the shadows. "What the—"

Maxwell's words cut off as he fell, hard, onto his back. His attacker put a knee on his chest and bore down on him, his left knee on Maxwell's right upper arm and his right hand pressing Maxwell's Adam's apple nearly to the back of his throat.

"Where is she?" Patrick Carrigan demanded in a sharp whisper. His shoulder was bandaged, and a sling hung around his neck, though at the moment his arm was free of it. "Where's April?"

Maxwell tried to talk but couldn't. Patrick let up on his throat just a little.

"She's . . . don't know where . . ."

"Is she alive! Has Coldwell gotten to her and killed her?"

How did Carrigan know it was Coldwell? The gunman had been under strict orders to reveal nothing, not his name, the details of his mission, nothing! The idea had been to get Patrick Carrigan dispatched as quickly as possible.

"No . . . no . . . I don't know . . . what you mean!"

Patrick pressed on his throat again, until Maxwell nearly passed out. Then he let up the pressure, allowing Maxwell to gasp for air and revive a little.

"Next time you hire a killer, Maxwell, you'd best hire one who knows how to keep his mouth shut. You'd best hire one who doesn't laugh and chortle and spill the whole story to you before he shoots you—and shoots pretty badly, I have to say. I suppose he thought he'd shot me through the heart. One shot, I fall, lie still, and he just laughs and walks away. Overconfident, Hank Coldwell is. I guess he believes his own reputation."

"I . . . don't know such a man . . ."

"The hell you don't! He was here today. I watched him come through the gate. And I watched him leave later with four others. Who are they?"

"How . . . did you get in?"

"Not important. What's important is that I am in, and unless you tell me where I can find April, you'll never get up from this spot. Ever."

"I don't know . . . where she is."

"Have you sent out Coldwell after her?"

Maxwell wanted to lie, but he couldn't. He could see it would not be believed. It would probably get him killed on the spot.

"Yes . . . yes!"

"Who are the others with him?"

"Hirelings . . . to help him . . ."

"Where are they going?"

"Her uncle . . . the mining camp . . . Chess, it's called."

Patrick Carrigan's eyes widened. "Of course! I should have thought of that myself! She always told me that she'd go there if ever she had trouble of any serious kind . . . her only refuge, she said. Other than me. Her only refuge."

Maxwell began to feel anger mixing with his terror. Against his better judgment he spat up at his antagonist: "A whore . . . she's but a whore . . . *my* whore! My property, not yours."

Patrick let go of Maxwell's neck long enough to strike him in the face with his fist, very hard. Maxwell's jawbone crunched. Patrick hit him again and he passed out.

Patrick Carrigan rose and paced back and forth near the unconscious man. He fought against panic. Five hired killers, on their way to do in the woman he loved . . . the woman who carried his child.

What could he do? One man alone, already wounded, bearing the pain of a gunshot shoulder only with a continual exertion of will . . . what could he do?

Maxwell moved, groaned. Patrick ignored him. Maxwell rolled over, reaching out toward something on the ground. Patrick, distracted, was only half-aware of this, and when he looked, it was too late.

Maxwell sliced a knife toward him, catching him in the calf. He grunted in pain and staggered back, the knife pulling free. Maxwell came to his feet and advanced, knife slashing.

Patrick dodged, then drove a punch directly into Maxwell's face. The nose crunched and crumbled. Maxwell let out a muffled yelp, blood flooding over his mouth. He slashed again. This time Patrick hit him in the throat, as hard as he could. Maxwell collapsed.

Patrick knew Maxwell was dead even before his examination of the body confirmed it. The realization numbed him. He'd just killed a man . . . and not just any man, but one of the most popular and influential men in the nation, a man everyone, friend or foe, assumed was destined for the presidency.

Patrick did not care that Maxwell was dead. He knew the man for the vile being he was . . . had learned that long before, soon after he and April fell in love and she confided to him her associations with

Maxwell. She had never wanted to become his mistress, had been forced into it by circumstances and even threats. She'd come to loathe Maxwell in time. When she spoke of him to Patrick, she said his name like it bore the taste of bile.

But Patrick knew that this death, unplanned and in self-defense as it was, threw up a huge barrier before him. Because of who this man was, his killing would be investigated in great detail.

Just now Patrick Carrigan had no room in his life for this kind of problem. He wanted only to get to April before Coldwell and his gang did.

As he thought through his situation, he realized that matters might not be dire for him regarding Maxwell's death. He and the corpse were at the moment not visible from the house because of the darkness, the grove of trees, and some conveniently placed shrubs. And nearby was a well, covered over and evidently not used. It had a look of incompleteness about it; probably it was a well that had proven out dry or otherwise unusable and been abandoned. A much larger and complete well was nearer the house; that was the one, he suspected, that was actually used.

He dragged the corpse to the well, scooted back the cover, and dropped the great Crane Hart Maxwell down into the hole. It thudded rather than splashed; the well was dry. But also deep. It would take some time for the corpse to be discovered there.

He put the cover back in place, brushed away his footprints, did the same in the grove area, then circled the wall, in the shadows, until he found a place where he could, with the help of a nearby tree, make his way to the top of the wall. He did so with great suffering because of his wounded shoulder, but determination was strong. He went over the wall and put the cdifice of the late Crane Hart Maxwell behind him forever.

21

"I don't know that I've ever felt a colder wind," Liam Carrigan said. He pulled his coat more tightly around him and looked down the barren street that was the main thoroughfare of the Chess mining camp. It was a somber place, empty, full of shadows and cobwebs and loose shutters that banged in the wind.

"And I don't know that I've ever seen a more dead town," Joseph replied. "Kind of ghostly hereabouts."

"It's what comes when a strike gives out," Liam replied. "No point in lingering when that happens."

"I hope my uncle has lingered," April said. "I hope he's still alive and well."

She dismounted and walked up beside Liam. "What if he doesn't want me?" she said.

"How could he not? You're his niece. His only remaining kin."

"I'm also carrying a baby, and I'm not married."

Liam looked at her several moments. "A good husband is important for a woman to have."

"Yes."

Liam opened his mouth, then closed it again, and looked away, saying no more.

April turned to go back toward the mule, tripped, and fell hard.

"April!" Joseph exclaimed, rushing to her even though Liam was already at her side and stooping to help her up. "Dear Lord, are you all right?"

"Calm down, Joseph," Liam said. "It was just a little fall."

"Little falls can make a difference to a woman with child," Joseph said. "April, do you think you're hurt?"

"Not at all," she said rising, with Joseph offering so much "help" that he actually made the process more difficult. "Liam's right . . . it was only a little fall."

"Don't be so panicky about everything, Joseph," Liam said. "Dang, you make a man jumpy just to watch you."

Joseph rose, turned, and walked away, staring out across a spectacular landscape, his back to Liam and April. April looked at him with concern, then went back to the mule.

Liam approached him and Joseph walked farther away. "Hold up, Joseph. Let me talk to you."

"Not in a talking humor right now." Joseph advanced farther, then rounded an empty cabin. Liam followed.

"Can't a man make some water without somebody trailing after him."

"You didn't come around here to make water. What the deuce is wrong with you, brother? You've been moping and growling half the day. And what's all this worrying to death about everything April does? She's healthy and strong. That baby isn't going to just fall out of her every time she gets a little jolt."

Joseph turned a glowering face to his brother. "Are you the authority on such things now?"

"No. It's just common sense. If women were that delicate, we'd have an empty world. No child would ever live long enough to be born."

To Liam's surprise, Joseph's eyes grew moist. "Some don't make it to be born," he said quietly. "And sometimes mothers don't make it through, either."

"What are you getting at?"

Joseph took a deep breath and studied the horizon again. "Liam, ever since we got back together after the war, you've gone on about how I'm like a preacher or a schoolmarm or an old grandmother."

"That's just because you get so dang moral on me sometimes. I can't so much as look at a woman without you acting like I've committed the unpardonable sin."

196

Joseph shook his head. "No. I don't think that. I know what the unpardonable sin is, Liam. And you're looking at the man who committed it."

"What are you talking about?"

"If I sometimes seem to get a little . . . wrought up over your consorting with women, your fornicating and such . . ."

"No reason to use such a strong word for it."

"It is what it is, no matter what you call it. My point, though, is that there's a reason I'm like I am about that. There was a time, when we'd parted ways there before the war started, that I . . . that there was a woman. Her name was Lydia. You never met her, never knew her. But Lydia, because of me, got into the same situation that April is in."

"You're telling me you fathered a child?"

"I did."

"Good Lord, Joe. Where is the child now?"

"With his mother." Joseph reached up and wiped a tear that streaked down his grimy face. "With his mother, lying in a grave back in Tennessee."

"I'll be damned."

"No . . . it's my fear that it'll be me who's damned. I fathered that child . . . in my own love and passion for Lydia, I got her with child and us not even married, and then I dawdled about, tried to persuade myself I had no obligation to her . . . I even prayed that it all would just go away. I

197

prayed that, Liam. And then it did go away. There were problems. I don't know what caused them. But when I was off, not there to help her like I should have been, she bled, and she died. She and her child both. Died alone. I've never forgotten what it was like to stand by that grave, Liam. And I'll never forget." He paused. "I don't know why I chose right now to tell you this. I never planned to tell you at all."

"Joseph, I don't know what to say."

"What you say doesn't matter so much as what you do. It's easy for a man to get carried away with a woman, or to treat a man's loving of a woman as a kind of pleasure sport. But it's not that way. It causes new lives to come about. It changes the life of the woman forever. It's not a light thing. It's not something you can walk away from, like I did. God, I wish I hadn't! Every day I think about it. Every day."

"So that's why you preach at me."

"That's why. I know the seriousness of it all, first-hand. What is a few minutes of pleasure for a man can bring a new life to a woman . . . and sometimes it can bring her death."

Liam said nothing. He turned and walked away, leaving Joseph alone.

"What's wrong?" April asked him when he reached her. "Is Joseph sick?"

"No. He'll be all right. Just give him a few minutes."

"Are you sure everything is all right?"

"I think everything will be fine. He's just got something weighing on him right now."

"Is there something we can do?"

"No. There's nothing."

The search for the way to Michael McCree's cabin was a rather random venture, because upon reaching the empty mining camp they had exhausted all the information they had. He was in the vicinity of the place, they knew, but where? Was there a road, or just a path? If the man was a hermit, did he deliberately take some unseen way to reach his home, so no one could find him?

Lacking answers, all they could do was search the area. And after three sweeps all around town, they were about ready to give up, but then Liam stopped.

"Take a look at that," he said. "Could be a path."

Joseph studied the area toward which Liam pointed. "Well, yes, it could be. Or maybe not . . . but it's the most likely thing we've found yet."

"April, is your uncle Michael the kind who will greet us with a shotgun or such as that?" Liam asked.

"Not if he knows it's me," she said. "If we find a cabin, let me do the talking."

"I can go along with that," Joseph said, with Liam nodding.

They led old Ben up the path, and the weary but patient mule plodded right along as usual. April walked, weary of riding and more sure of her own footing than that of the mule. It soon became evident that this truly was a path. The farther they traveled, the more trodden it appeared. April began to grow excited, and all of them quickened the pace, until Ben vetoed the move by refusing to move any faster than he was.

"Look!" Liam said, pointing ahead.

Through a gap in the trees a cabin wall showed. Round logs, saddle-notched, bark still on them. Not a highly finished out cabin, obviously, but stout and tightly chinked.

"That has to be it," Joseph said.

"I'll call to him," April said. "Just in case."

She advanced a few paces, put her hand to her mouth, and called: "Michael! Uncle Michael! It's me . . . April!"

The wind whispered through the trees to answer her, but that was the only answer she received.

"Uncle Michael? Are you there?"

Silence. She turned and looked at the Carrigan brothers, troubled.

"I hope he's all right."

"He's probably just away," Joseph said.

"Should we go on in closer, or wait?" asked Liam.

"Let's leave that up to April."

She thought about it a few moments. "I think we can go on in. Not into the cabin, just the clearing. We'll wait for him out in the open, so he can see right away that it's me."

"How long since he's seen you?"

"I was thirteen, maybe fourteen."

"You'll have changed a lot."

"He'll know me. I'm sure of it."

They advanced on in. The cabin yard was bare dirt, well packed. There was a log privy, which Liam visited, and a few sheds and lean-tos. But all about the scene a pall of intense silence hung, and a sense that this was a place that perhaps had not been visited by human presence for quite some time.

April walked slowly about, thoughtful. Joseph brooded over near the woodshed, and Liam nosed about here and there, curious as a boy.

"Take a look at this!" he said, kicking at a wooden panel being used as part of a lean-to shelter. "Looks like the side panel of some kind of show wagon. You can see the paint, pictures, and words and all. Mighty weathered, though. Let's see: 'See the Amazing . . . the Amazing . . .' No. Can't make it out."

"Does your uncle have a history as a showman?" Joseph asked April.

"No. Not to my knowledge."

"Yeah," Liam said. "Being a showman and a hermit at the same time doesn't quite seem to fit. I guess he just picked up the panel in town or something, and made use of it."

Joseph paced about, and neared the front of the cabin. He noted a shutter partially open and glanced inside. He stared into the darkness, unmoving, then glanced over his shoulder. April was looking off at clouds rolling over the peaks, and watching smoke rise in the distance from the chimneys of the mining community of Brasstown.

Joseph caught Liam's eye and gestured subtly for him to come over. Liam did so, quietly.

"Take a look through the window and tell me if you see what I think I see," Joseph said softly.

Liam looked, then got a little closer and looked all the harder. He turned and faced Joseph with a somber expression.

"Wonder what killed him?"

"Shot himself, I guess. Though how he could do that and not fling the pistol is beyond me."

"You want to tell her, or me?"

"I guess we should do it together."

"It's going to be hard on her."

"I know."

22

Liam couldn't help but stare, for this was a sight a man would probably see once in his lifetime, if that. It wasn't pretty to look at, but once seen, it was hard to look away.

April knelt beside the table, looking sadly at the drawn and dried leather thing that once had been her uncle. He was fully clothed—not in miner's clothing, oddly, but more in a cattleman's garb— and his hat sat on his head, cocked back so his full brow was exposed. His eyes were closed, the lids shriveled down over the place orbs used to be, and his lips were drawn back to reveal yellowed, worn-down teeth. He was the color of a long-used saddle. Strangest of all, he gripped a pistol in his right hand, not lying flat, but sitting upright, like he'd propped it on the table to shoot a hole in the far wall.

The presence of the pistol had naturally roused suspicions of suicide, but Joseph's close investigation of the body showed no evidence of a bullet wound. Clearly he'd not shot himself in the head, for that would have had a very visible effect, but neither was there any powder burn or hole on his coat or vest to indicate a self-inflicted shot through the heart or other vitals.

And how the devil had he managed to keep hold of the pistol, anyway?

"I'm mighty sorry, April," Liam said. "I'd have liked to get to know him."

"He was a good man," she said, wiping away a tear. "It's just so sad that he's gone. Do you think he killed himself?"

"You know what I think?" Joseph said, winging it as he spoke. "I think . . . I think he was probably cleaning that pistol, had it out to look at it, and just died. Probably his heart. Just died, sitting right there, peaceful and comfortable. That would explain why there's no wound."

Liam gently pried the revolver from the rigid hand. "I'll be . . . not a bullet fired. Every chamber is loaded with live ammunition. So he didn't shoot himself at all."

"There you go," Joseph said. "It had to be a peaceful passing, then. He just sat down and died."

"I'm glad he didn't suffer," April said. "Put the pistol back in his hand, Liam. It bothers me to see his hand all clawed out like that."

Liam put the pistol back in place.

"Should we bury him?" Joseph asked April.

"Not yet. Just let him sit there. He looks . . . peaceful."

A peaceful hunk of well-cured leather is what he really looks like, Liam thought.

"Amazing that he mummified like that," Joseph observed. "I wonder what caused it? The high altitude, maybe?"

"You'd halfway think he'd been salted down like a ham," Liam said. When he noted April giving him a reproving look, he muttered an apology.

"We'll leave him for now, April, if that's what you want," Joseph said. "I guess he has every right to be here. It's his place, after all."

"He seems so much smaller than I remember him," April said.

"I guess when you dry out a person you get the same kind of results as when you dry out a grape," Liam said. "Sort of a human raisin."

Both Joseph and April frowned at him. Liam reddened and turned away. "Guess I should just shut up."

"Good idea."

"I wonder if there's any food around here that's still good?" he asked, and began looking through the shelves.

April went to the bed, removed the sheet, and

draped it over the dead man. Liam glanced back and was startled. "Lord! Looks like a ghost!" he said. "April, you sure you don't want us to go ahead and dig a hole and bury him?"

"Tomorrow."

"It won't bother you, having your dead uncle sitting at the table while you sleep tonight?"

"He's my uncle," she said. "Why should it bother me? It'll give me a chance to tell him good-bye."

Joseph was close enough for Liam to whisper to at that moment. "Let's just hope he doesn't tell her good-bye back. If he does, I'm running through that wall yonder."

They found flour—surprisingly fresh—and shortening and so on. Bacon, too, and coffee—again, surprisingly fresh. "This mountain air must really preserve things," Liam observed.

Joseph made biscuits while Liam began frying thick rashers of bacon. April boiled strong coffee, found some potatoes, and cut them up to boil.

"Your uncle Michael kept a well-stocked larder," Joseph observed.

"I'm amazed by it, really," April said. "Mostly by how things haven't deteriorated. Is it possible that a person could . . . mummify that way in only a few days?"

"Maybe so. The world is full of mysteries," Liam said. "I read a story once about a man who accidentally got pickled."

"You're joshing," Joseph said.

"No, no. Pickled up like a big old cucumber."

Though they had made a tentative short-term peace with the dead man at the table, none of them could quite work up the will to sit there to eat. They scattered around the cabin, Liam on the floor, Joseph in a chair, April reclining on a sort of homemade sofa that must have been a creation of her uncle's. The food was filling, hot, delicious. The weary travelers soon felt quite content and sated. Liam tilted down his hat, as was his habit, and dropped into a quick nap, leaning against the wall.

Joseph dozed off, too, propping his splinted hand on the armrest of the chair. It was sore in the bones, and he fell asleep worrying that injuring the hand had triggered some sort of latent rheumatism. April remained alert a little longer than the men, looking at her sheet-covered uncle and grieving that he had not lived to greet her; then she, too, began to nod and finally to slumber.

The sun declined westward and night began to steal over the land.

"April?"

The voice came from the murky borderlands of sleep. April murmured, stirred. Joseph and Liam, also hearing the voice, did the same.

"April, honey, is that really you?"

She jolted up to a sitting position. Joseph and Liam did the same, Liam swearing loudly and groping for his pistol.

The man who'd just entered raised a lever-action Henry and aimed it at Liam. "Hold still, there, companion."

April rose. "Uncle Michael?"

"April! It is you! Glory be!"

She rushed to him and threw her arms around him. He smiled and hugged her with one arm, struggling at the same time to keep the rifle trained on Liam.

"April, child, where in the world did you come from? What brings you? And who are these two?"

She kissed him hard on his whiskered cheek, and he gave up trying to keep the rifle trained. He laid it at his feet and threw both arms around his niece, hugging her close. He was broad and bearded and clad in a buffalo coat, and from the perspective of the Carrigan brothers, it looked like she was being embraced by a huge bear.

"Honey, I don't know why you're here, but I'm glad to see you. But tell me: Why have you throwed a sheet over the Colonel?"

"We thought it was you, Uncle Michael. We thought you'd died and dried up in your chair."

He roared with laughter. "The Colonel will think

that's a good one. Me, being him? I'm a bear, he's a pruned-up shrimp! Ha!"

He hugged her again.

Michael McCree listened well. And for someone who chose to live his life far from the company of others, grubbing out what little livelihood he could from mines that all others had abandoned as useless, he was a jovial and welcoming host.

The Carrigan brothers won his favor quickly, both for being Irishmen, and for the friendship and protection they'd given to April. He pumped both their hands and even hugged Joseph, nearly crushing him. He was a big, earthy man with a big, earthy smell. Joseph came out of the embrace with essence of Michael McCree permeating his clothing.

April told the story, mincing no words, sparing no details, laying out her own situation with full honesty and no attempt to enwrap herself in sainthood. "I'm carrying a child, and I'm not married," she said flatly as she summarized at the end of her narrative. "I'm in danger, and I need a place to hide until I can have my baby and find some other option. I don't know that Crane Maxwell will ever give up trying to get rid of me. I betrayed him by loving someone else. And he is afraid, too, that the child is his own, and that poses a danger to his reputation.

A president does not need a bastard child roaming out there in the country somewhere."

"April, I ain't no man to judge others. Judge not that ye be not judged, that's my motto. If you've done bad in the past, you ain't the first one, and you won't be the last one, and I figure let them that is without sin cast the first stone. Ain't that right, Irish companions? Huh?"

"Amen, brother," Liam said.

"You stay here as long as you want. Forever, if you want to. I'll help you raise that there baby. We'll turn it into a fine strapping fellow, or if it's a girl, we'll get her pretty frock dresses and I'll carve her play-pretty dolls out of wood. And if Maxwell sends any trouble to us—which he won't because how the devil would he find us?—we'll throw them a hot lead reception." He turned and spoke to the corpse at the table, uncovered again and still aiming that pistol at whoever happened to get in front of it. "What do you say to that, Colonel? You want to help us raise a baby? Huh?" He grinned at April. "The Colonel likes the notion."

Joseph asked, "Mr. McCree, I've got to—"

"Ain't no 'mister,' just Michael. Big Michael the hermit! That's what I'm called down in Brasstown. Anyway, you got to what?"

"I've got to ask you: Who is the Colonel and how'd he come to be here . . . like he is?"

"Well, that's an odd story, that one. I don't know if the Colonel wants me to tell it in front of him, because he's sensitive about how he come to be dead. And he's a little shaken by the story little April just told, it including reference to the very man who took his life."

"What do you mean?" Liam asked.

"The Colonel there is a famous man on two counts. The first is that he was one wicked devil of a gunman in his day. The second is that he was the first man ever known killed by none other than the infamous Hank Coldwell."

Liam rose and walked to the corpse, kneeling beside it and studying the face. "Colonel Bishop, sure as the world! That's him!"

"It is indeed. The one and only."

"Wait a minute," Joseph said. "That's Colonel Bishop, the gunfighter?"

"That's the man. And that's the pistol he killed twenty-three other pistoleers with, until somebody hired a man named Hank Coldwell to get rid of him. Coldwell shot him through the heart three times. If you were to look under the Colonel's shirt, you'd see the three holes in him. But don't look. He's sensitive about that."

"Why is he mummified . . . and here?"

"Let me take a guess," Liam said. "I read something about this in a newspaper once. There's some fellow who took the Colonel's body after he died, stole it right off an undertaker's slab, and had it salted down and dried out and so on. Then he took him out in a show wagon across the west, showing the body off for a fee."

"You got it right, Liam," McCree said. "'See the Amazing Mummy of Colonel Bishop, Famed Gunfighter! See the Pistol that Spat Death at Twenty-Three Desperate Men!' That was what was written on the side of the wagon. I've got that panel out there in use on a lean-to right now, though you can't much read it anymore."

"We saw it," Liam said. "Was it you who traveled around with the corpse?"

"Lord, no. But the fellow who did come to Brasstown a few years ago and up and died right there. I sort of adopted the Colonel, brung him up here to join me."

"Why?"

"Dang, boys, it gets lonesome up here! Even a hermit needs a little company. The Colonel, he makes for a good house companion. A fine listener, that man is, and slow to give advice you don't want to hear."

"Amazing," Joseph said.

"He is, ain't he!" Michael McCree grinned, flashing coffee-colored teeth.

"He doesn't ever make you feel . . . skittish or crawly?" Liam asked. "You know what I mean."

"Why, no. The Colonel is good company. Good company."

"Why did they call him the Colonel?" Joseph asked. "Was he a military man?"

"Pshaw! He was a deserter out of the Reb army! Ain't that right, Colonel? They call him the Colonel because his first name is Colonel. No rank, just a name. But I never figured how his mother years ago looked down at her pink wiggling baby and thunk, 'I think I'll call him Colonel.' Just can't picture that in my head, but it happened. Hey, how long can you boys stay here?"

Liam and Joseph looked at one another and shrugged. "Well, I don't know. We were bound for Montana, looking for our uncle there, when all this happened. We're a little sidetracked . . . I suppose there's no particular schedule for us."

"Winter will roll in here soon. Stay the winter with us. You fellows good hunters? Help me keep meat on the table?"

"We could do that," Liam said. Joseph grunted agreement.

"Can you work a mine?"

"We can do anything," Liam said. "We've gone broke doing every kind of job you can think of."

"Ha! Don't I know what you mean! By all rights I should do what everybody else has and leave this place. Just too stubborn to do it. And it don't take much to keep an old lonely fellow like me alive. And the Colonel, he don't eat much. Right, Colonel? Right."

"Can you make it back and forth to Brasstown during the winter?" Joseph asked.

"You can on snowshoes. The sliding kind going down, the walking kind coming back up. I use them when I've got to get to town, which I don't bother doing much come winter."

"Maybe Liam and I could find work in Brasstown. Tending bar or sweeping floors or something."

"Maybe so. But things get slow there come the cold months. May not be jobs. But it don't matter. A man can work a mine even in the cold. You can help me out. I'm on the verge of a big strike, companions. These old mines ain't as give out as people thunk when they pulled out! And even if we don't hit the strike, we'll make it through. All it takes is shelter, firewood, and enough food, and we can manage that. No problem."

"I guess we stay, then," Liam said. "If Joseph is willing, and April doesn't mind living in a little house with three men."

"I don't mind," she said. "I'd feel honored and safe to have you all here."

"What money we've got, Michael, we'll use to lay in more supplies," Joseph said.

"We'll add a room to the house, just for April and the baby," Michael said. "That's the good thing about cabins. Easy to make them bigger. Dang, this is going to work out fine! You boys, me, you, April, and the Colonel! *There's* a party!"

"You're mighty sociable for a man who chooses to live alone," Liam observed.

"The problem ain't me wanting to be away from folks. It's just that people can't hardly stand living with me. I can't figure it out. The Colonel's the only one who can put up with me."

"That's because he can't smell," April said. "Do you own a bathtub, Uncle Michael?"

"I got a tin washtub."

"Tonight we'll put it to use. I want to raise my baby around clean and sweet-smelling people."

McCree's smile weakened but did not vanish. "Well . . . I guess having my niece here with me is worth some sacrifice. You going to make the Colonel bathe, too?"

"No. I think the Colonel is fine just like he is. I'm inclined not to bother him."

"There's something we can't forget here," Joseph said. "We may draw trouble up to this mountain, Michael. If Maxwell should somehow track us down, he might send someone after us. Maybe even Coldwell again, the Colonel's old friend."

"Send him on," McCree said without hesitation. "We'll show them an Irish welcome, right, companions?"

His confidence was contagious. Liam and Joseph grinned as one. "Right," Joseph said.

23

Ben, as always, plodded along at one pace, heavy hooves thumping the mountainside as Joseph and Liam made their way down toward Brasstown. In their pockets was all the money they had, and they would spend almost all of it on supplies. April remained at the cabin with her uncle and the Colonel, resting, eating, regaining strength after her long ordeals. Among the items on the supply list in Joseph's pocket was cloth, needle, and thread, to be used by April to make clothing for herself, and for her baby. She'd already declared that, if it was a boy, she would name him Patrick. And his middle name would be Michael, after his uncle.

Hard at work for two days now cutting and notching trees to expand the cabin, and gathering stone to use in building a new fireplace in the room, Michael also remained at the cabin. He was already planning how best to construct a shield for the fireplace so that his great-niece or great-nephew wouldn't someday accidentally toddle into the fire.

"We've got some things to work out, you and me," Liam said, as he and Joseph hiked along. "We both love her, and we both can't have her."

"That's not correct," Joseph replied.

"What? How can two men have the same woman?"

"My point is that we both love her, but she doesn't love us. Not in the way you're talking about. She's still in love with Patrick Carrigan."

"But he's dead."

"Not to her. He may be dead to the world, but it will take a long time before he'll die to her. You and I may as well get over being smitten, Liam. Neither one of us will wind up with her. All we'll do is spend a winter competing with each other, getting to not like each other, fussing and fighting and feuding worse than we ever have, and in the end it will all have been for nothing, because she's not going to have either one of us. The only Carrigan she wants is the one she can't possibly have."

"You're a pessimist, Joseph. I think I could persuade that girl to fall in love with me."

"You've always had a lot of confidence, Liam. In my thinking the Colonel's probably got as much chance with her as you or I have."

"Speaking of the Colonel, you know what's really

strange about having a dead man living with you like that?"

"The whole thing is strange."

"Yeah . . . but the really strange part is, I'm getting used to it. I'm actually talking to the Colonel sometimes, and not thinking anything odd about it."

"It's the mountains. They bring out the oddness in folks."

"That's got to be it."

"I wonder if it bothers April to see the Colonel every day and know he died at the hands of the same man who killed her lover, and tried hard to kill her?"

"I've had the same question in my mind. If it bothers her, she doesn't show it. Maybe she just hasn't thought much about that aspect of it."

"I think it's because she's just so strong. What she's gone through would wipe out a lot of folks, but she just holds up and keeps going for the sake of that baby."

"God bless her for it, I say. And God keep Hank Coldwell and Crane Hart Maxwell and all his ilk far, far away from her. And us."

"It may not happen, Joseph."

"Why do you say that?"

"April admitted something to me yesterday. She admitted that she's mentioned her uncle in Chess, Colorado, to Maxwell in the past. She's worried that he might figure out she's come here."

Joseph mulled it over. "That worries me a little, too."

"Let's buy some extra ammunition in town today. Just in case."

"That's a good idea."

Most of what they required they found at a big general store in the heart of town. The storekeeper was a friendly fellow, but quite curious, inquisitive in a well-intentioned way about who the Carrigans were, where they were living, and so on. It wasn't common for folks to move to the high mountains in the wintertime, he told them. Usually folks wintered in lower climes during cold weather and came to the mountains in the spring. They gave only cagey, indirect answers. Given the chance that they might be tracked down, it was best not to have it known precisely where they lived. A talkative and unsuspecting shopkeeper could be a source of dangerous information if plied by one such as Hank Coldwell.

The brothers split up after leaving the general store, Joseph heading for the gun shop to buy ammunition and Liam going to the saddle shop to obtain some leather strapping that Michael McCree wanted. When he'd made that purchase, he plodded through town to rejoin Joseph, but paused when he passed a saloon.

Liam still had some money in his pocket, and it couldn't hurt to have a few extra bottles of whiskey to see them through the winter. And a drink to enjoy today, right now.

He entered, made his purchases. He left with five bottles of whiskey wrapped in paper and stowed in a cloth sack, two shots of whiskey warming his belly, and Hank Coldwell and Kirby Boone on his trail.

"I knew they'd show themselves sooner or later if they were here," Coldwell said to Boone, the one man among his new gang whom he'd come to like, a little. The others he despised and would gladly dispatch with a bullet in the brain pan should the opportunity arise. He hoped it would.

"So what now? We track them?"

"That's right. The girl isn't with them, and she's the one Maxwell wants the most. We'll let them lead us to her."

"I'm not sure this is worthwhile anymore," Boone said. "Not since that telegram."

The reference was to a message received the day before after Coldwell wired in to Maxwell to inform him they were in Brasstown and optimistic of locating their prey. The reply telegram had come from Halforth and informed them that Maxwell was inexplicably missing, and fears were growing that something had happened to him. He'd not been known to vanish in this manner before.

"You figure Maxwell is dead, huh, and won't be paying us?"

"That's what I figure."

"If he's dead, we'll get paid anyway. I'll see to that. Halforth is a weakling and coward, and I'll persuade him very easily to pay up out of Maxwell's coffers. And the truth is, I don't care that much about the money, myself. This thing is personal now. I want to watch those Carrigan brothers squirm while I kill them, slowly. And I want the girl's head on a stick."

"Looks like you'll get your chance. Is that the other brother there?"

Joseph had just emerged from the gun shop. Liam was talking to him, holding up the sack with the whiskey.

"That's him." They stepped into a recessed doorway to avoid being spotted. "Go round up the others," Coldwell said. "We've got some following to do."

Just a glimpse, that was all. A flash of movement, a hint of a face . . . Coldwell wasn't even quite sure he'd seen it. He'd experienced incidents like this before, though he never told anyone about them: glimpses of a figure in a crowd, looking at him through the eyes of someone who died at his hand; cold fingers brushing his brow as he fell asleep and the fading impression of familiar phantom faces looking down at him when he jerked awake; voices whispering out of corners where no one was, voices of those he had killed, usually saying one word over and over: guilt, guilt, guilt, guilt . . .

"What is it, Coldwell?" asked Pap Grimmer, eldest of the Maxwell-assembled gang and the man among them most antagonistic to Coldwell. Coldwell already had plans to inflict a particularly unpleasant death upon the old fellow once they had the Carrigan brothers out of the way and the girl ready for her grave.

"Somebody there, behind that old store building."

"Ain't nobody there."

"There was."

"He's right," said shotgun-toting Rodney Elton from behind his thick circular glasses. "I seen it, too."

"Hell, with your eyes what you see don't count."

"I'm telling you, there's somebody back there," Elton insisted.

"Damned fools," Grimmer spat.

"Calm down, Pap. It can't hurt to check it out," said Pete Wayne in his strong Indiana accent.

"I'll go," Elton said. He edged toward the back of the building slowly, shotgun ready. He paused, then wheeled to sweep the area behind the building with his shotgun.

He quickly lowered it. "Nobody here."

"There he goes!" Wayne exclaimed, pointing northeast.

They all saw him then, a lone figure, carrying a rifle in his right hand. His left arm and shoulder were bandaged.

"Who is he?" Grimmer asked.

"Don't know," Wayne said. "Anybody know him?"

A combined chorus of grunted negatives . . . from all but Coldwell.

"You know him, Coldwell?"

"No."

"What's wrong with you? You look a little pale. Seeing a ghost, are you?"

"Hell, no. Now shut up, and let's go get him. Split up, you two around that way, you two the other way. I'll head up the middle."

They divided. With his pistol drawn, Coldwell advanced up the street, keeping sheltered as best he could beneath porch overhangs and in recessed doorways. As soon as he was out of sight of the others, however, he ducked into an empty church building and leaned against the wall, panting and panicked.

The face he'd seen was that of Pat Carrigan, the man he would have sworn was dead out on the Missouri plains. So Maxwell had been right after all! Carrigan had survived.

And now he was here, probably to protect the girl.

Coldwell closed his eyes, feeling a familiar warning inside his head, that demon that pounded at his skull and told him a seizure was imminent. He fought it, tried to push it back . . .

Outside a gunshot sounded and he heard a horrific screech, a man crying out in a high and pitiful voice.

Joseph and Liam heard the shot as well. They were well up the trail, almost to the house. They looked at each other, knowing what it probably meant.

Other shots sounded. They came from below, down in the ghost town of Chess.

"Go on up . . . warn Michael and April," Liam said. "I'll go down and see what's happening."

"No need to go up and warn them. They'll have heard the shots, too."

"Good point. Joseph, if it's Coldwell, who would he be shooting at? We're up here, and Michael and April as well."

"Maybe Michael is down there, and we just don't know it. Maybe he went to scrounge wood for expanding the cabin."

"If that's so, then April is up in the house alone."

"You go see that she's all right. I'll go down."

"No. You go to her. I'll go to the fight."

More gunshots. Liam yanked out a coin and

flipped it. "Heads I go to the fight, tails you go to April." He flipped it fast and showed it to Joseph. "Tails. You go to April."

Grabbing his rifle from off the pack mule and checking to ensure he had plenty of ammunition, Liam said a quick farewell and turned to trot back down toward Chess.

"I'll join you as quick as I see she's safe," Joseph said.

"No! You stay with her to protect her if you have to!" Then Liam was out of sight.

Joseph hurried up toward the house. Then it hit him: Heads, Liam goes to the fight, tails, Joseph goes to the house . . . either way, it's Liam in the gunfight.

The clever devil had taken advantage of the confusion to slip one right past the usually astute Joseph Carrigan. Joseph would have words with him about that later.

He had just reached the house when Michael appeared, Henry rifle in hand. "What the devil's going on down in the town?"

"Liam's gone down to see . . . I'm going, too, now that I know you're here to protect April. We thought it might be Coldwell, shooting at you."

"Not me, companion. I'll go with you."

"I'll go. Somebody should stay and defend the house."

"You do it. That's my mining camp down there, by jingo! Ain't nobody going to gunfight in it without me knowing the tall and short of it." With that, he ran heavily past Joseph and on down the trail toward Chess.

Joseph took Ben to the barn, got his own rifle off the pack and a supply of ammunition. He'd unload the mule later. For now it was time to make sure April was all right, and set up a defense.

He prayed for Liam and Michael. Even as he whispered the words, more gunfire erupted down in the empty mining camp.

24

Despite the crispness of the air, Liam was perspiring, every muscle tensed. At the edge of town, he hid behind what was once a saloon and listened to the sudden onslaught of silence that had descended upon Chess.

What did it mean? Was it over? Who had prevailed—for that matter, who had fought?

He edged around the back of the old saloon and peered through a gap between log buildings. On the dirt street beyond he saw nothing but an old mercantile store sign swinging and creaking on its post, but through an open window in the building just to his left he saw someone move and caught a glimpse of a rifle barrel.

There was a back door, open. He slipped to it and peered around into the inside of the building.

No one. But he hadn't imagined what he'd seen. He squinted, looking harder.

A figure loomed before him, coming from the side and leveling a rifle at him. Liam raised his own rifle, but something kept him from squeezing the trigger.

Neither did the man facing him fire. They looked at one another, and it struck Liam why he hadn't fired.

The fellow looked a lot like Joseph, and a bit like Liam himself, for that matter.

He had a bandaged shoulder and an arm sling that at the moment wasn't in use. Liam played what seemed to him a most impossible hunch.

"Your name wouldn't be Carrigan, would it?"

"It is. Pat Carrigan. And yours . . ."

"Liam Carrigan. Son of your father's younger brother, as I understand things. But I believed you to be dead."

"How do you know me?"

"My brother Joseph and I have been watching out for April. She's alive and well, and up in a cabin above here, with Joseph guarding her."

Patrick Carrigan looked like he might faint from relief. "Thank God."

"How did you survive? We've believed that Hank Coldwell killed you."

"He shot me . . . believed he killed me. He didn't."

"So I see." Liam had his rifle in his right hand and stuck out his left for a shake. "You been shot today, Pat?"

"Shot at but not hit. It's been lively, though. Right now they don't know where I am, I don't believe. As best I can count, there's five of them, one of them being Coldwell."

"Let's see if we can't put him out of our misery today, cousin I never knew I had."

"I agree. You say April is well?"

"Fine. Her baby, too."

"I'm grateful."

Liam looked past Patrick all at once. "Duck!" he yelled.

Patrick Carrigan obeyed at once. Liam raised his rifle and fired at the figure that had just appeared in the front doorway of the empty building. His shot struck the man in the center of his chest and drove him back. The shotgun he'd been about to empty at the back of Patrick Carrigan went flying one direction and his glasses flew from his face in the other. The shotgun landed, went off, and splintered the swinging mercantile sign with a blast of pellets.

"Wonder who that was?" Patrick said.

"I don't know, but likely he counts Crane Maxwell among his friends."

"Crane Maxwell is no longer a friend to any man."

"What's that mean?"

"I'd best not say."

An explosion of gunfire erupted on the other side of the little mining camp. "Come on, Pat," Liam said.

"There's a strong likelihood that there's another good man in this camp right now, trying to protect his niece. Let's go find him."

Neither man had time to analyze or even particularly take note of the bond that had formed between them almost instantly. Had they done so, they would have put it down to a simple fact: family. They were of the same blood, and had sensed it even if they did not really know it, from the instant they met.

Patrick came out of the back door, and he and Liam ran together up the alley, then across the street, Patrick stepping over the corpse of Rodney Elton. Patrick swept up the dropped shotgun, only one barrel of which had discharged. It was an instinctive move, not really planned, but a moment later he was glad he'd done it.

From behind a cabin came Pete Wayne, pistol expert, his Colt blasting. He'd aimed at Patrick's chest, but had miscalculated in allowing for Patrick's motion. The bullet hit the barrel of Patrick's pistol and sent it spinning out of his hand, leaving his hand instantly numb.

He reacted swiftly, lifting the shotgun, aiming it in the general direction of Wayne, and firing just as Wayne was about to squeeze off a second shot.

The buckshot struck Wayne in his extended pistol hand, knocking the pistol spinning and turning the hand and upper arm into a very ugly sampling of shredded meat. The remainder of the buckshot hit his face and made it disappear. He was dead before he hit the ground.

"Two out of five down," Liam said. "If you see a fellow in a buffalo coat, big bearish man with a beard and a Henry rifle, don't shoot him. That'd be Michael McCree."

"I've heard April talk of him many times. She always wanted to come see him."

"Not under these circumstances, I'll wager."

At that moment, Pap Grimmer stuck his pistol out a nearby window and fired. Patrick Carrigan let out a grunt and fell.

Grimmer swung his pistol and aimed at Liam at nearly point-blank range, then squeezed the trigger.

April huddled in the cabin, holding a rifle that Joseph had given her from Michael's gun rack.

"Still shooting," she whispered. "Still fighting. Because of me."

"No. Because Crane Hart Maxwell is an evil man," Joseph said. "Amazing, that he'd send men this far to get you."

"I'm a threat to him and his future."

"Which is all that matters to him. Can you imagine, April, what a bad thing it would be for such a man ever to reach the presidency?"

"It must not happen."

More gunfire. Joseph reflexively lunged toward the door, but pulled back, swearing softly to himself.

"Go on, Joseph. I know you want to fight. I know it's killing you to stay here."

"Somebody needs to remain here with you."

"I'm not a child."

"You're carrying one."

"And I can protect it, and myself. I have this rifle, and if I have to, I can take the pistol out of the Colonel's hand and use it. It's loaded."

Joseph bit his lip, struggling with himself. More gunshots, and the sound of a dinner bell ringing sharply, one time, probably hit by a stray bullet.

"I've got to go, April. If we can stop them down there, they'll never come up as far as this. If they do, show them no mercy. Kill them on sight, and don't hesitate, not even for a moment. If you do . . . well, it won't be what you want to have happen."

"I'll do what I must. Now go. And Joseph . . ." She grabbed him, pulled his face to hers, and kissed him on the mouth.

He gazed at her, stunned.

"I've wanted to do that since the first time I saw you."

He warmed inside, but she went on: "And Liam, too. You both remind me so much of Patrick."

Joseph smiled at her, and nodded, and knew at that moment that indeed there would be no chance for any relationship between him and this woman, or Liam and this woman. The earlier assessment was correct: Her love was still for the man she had lost and would not soon be redirected, if ever.

Joseph left the house and headed down the trail toward the ghost town.

Halfway down, his approach was seen by a man coming up the path. Hank Coldwell ducked behind some boulders and cocked his pistol, grinning at the thought of putting an end to the life of the same man who, in his view, had killed Sam Leisure. But he restrained himself from firing when he realized that April McCree, who was bound to be in that cabin he could clearly see, would hear the shot and realize it was fired very close to her refuge. To shoot Joseph now would be to forewarn her.

Later, then. He'd take care of her first, then the Carrigan brothers . . . if his partners below didn't take care of the task for him. He wished them luck. He didn't care just now who killed them, as long as they were killed.

Forever after the moment that Pap Grimmer pulled the trigger mere feet from his face, Liam Carrigan would be a much more religious man. He could not account for the failure of the pistol to discharge without assuming it had to be divine providence.

Liam reacted quickly to the turn of events. He

lunged forward and grabbed the pistol by the barrel, turning it upward. The next chamber was loaded and fired loudly, nearly deafening Liam, but the bullet flew into the sky. Liam punched with his left hand and hit Grimmer in the jaw. The old man fell backward, losing his pistol.

Patrick Carrigan, who Liam had thought was gunned down, sprang back up. The bullet had been fired in haste and had merely clipped his ankle. He leaped through the window and landed atop Grimmer, punched him fully in the face, twice. Grimmer struggled to reach his sheathed bowie knife, but Patrick sensed what he was doing and got it first. Grimmer managed to get a fist up and hit Patrick on the chin, but Patrick would not be moved. He brought the knife down and drove it into Grimmer's dark heart.

The old man made a wheezing sound and died. Patrick stood, leaving the knife still in him.

"I hate to do that to an old man," he said.

"Hey, Satan's old, but if you get a chance to kill him, then kill him. Come on . . . let's see who else might be roaming around this place."

"I want to get my hands on Coldwell," Patrick said.

"That's far enough, grizzly man."

Michael McCree winced as he heard the voice behind him. He'd been bent over, peering through a crack in the wall of a cabin, and the man had sneaked up behind him.

"Drop the Henry, big boy. No tricks."

He did so. "Can I turn around?" he said. "I'd like to at least see the face of the man who is going to kill me."

"Turn around. Say hello to Kirby Boone."

Michael turned slowly, hands still raised. "You the Kirby Boone that helped shoot up the town of Algood Springs back about '64?"

"That's me. Made me kind of famous, didn't it! That was quite a busy day, that one."

"Busy day for butchers of women and children."

"Hey, a man does what he has to do. Sorry that I have to kill you. You're quite a big rascal . . . kind of a shame to kill a man who's done such a job of growing. Kind of makes me want to let you go . . . like throwing back the monster fish of the pond if you're lucky enough to hook him."

"I'd not object to being let go free."

"Can't do it, friend." Kirby raised his pistol, a heavily modified Navy Colt, and aimed it at McCree's forehead.

"Between the eyes . . . that's where I like to put the bullet. Right in the square middle."

"I prefer a shot in the area of the ear, myself," McCree said.

"Well, being as how I sort of like you, I reckon I can oblige you if you want to take it there."

"Nah. I'll let you be the one."

Joseph Carrigan's bullet indeed did catch Kirby Boone in the ear, penetrating slightly upward through the brain and out the other side of the skull. Boone was dead before he had time to realize he'd been shot.

Joseph lowered his rifle. "Looks like I made it just in time," he said.

"That you did. I ought to scold you for leaving April, though."

"I had to come."

"I know. That's why I ain't scolding. That, and the fact you saved my skin."

"Listen . . . no more shooting."

"Maybe we got them all . . . or maybe whoever's left has gotten the rest of us."

"Let's do some exploring," Joseph said, levering another cartridge into his rifle's chamber.

They had just circled around cautiously onto what was a mining camp's version of a main street when they heard the sound of a gunshot, blasting, then echoing.

"That came from the house," McCree said.

"April . . ." Joseph felt a wave of sickness pass through him, and he struggled to keep his knees from giving way.

They turned and ran together. At the same moment, Liam emerged from an alley, and with him a man neither Joseph nor McCree had seen before.

Hank Coldwell smiled at April McCree and held up the rifle he'd snatched from her grasp just as she fired a shot at him. For a man of his size and age, already winded from his hike up from Chess, it had been quite a deft move, one that surprised her.

"Well, little missy, we meet again at last, and this time on terms I think I like. I'll hand it to you . . . you've run far and well, and this might seem a fine hiding place . . . but let me tell you something about hiding places. It's best not to tell where your chosen refuges are to the person who is trying to find you. Maxwell said he believed you would come here, as much as you spoke of it. And clearly he was right!"

"Leave me alone . . . my uncle is coming, and Liam and Joseph Carrigan . . . they'll kill you!"

"They'll not be back. My men below have taken care of that matter for good."

"I don't believe you."

"I saw them all die, with my own eyes. Except your uncle . . . he held on. The others are having some fun with him now. If you listen hard, maybe you'll hear him screaming."

"I don't believe you."

"Believe this—it ends for you right here. You

should have been a lot easier to kill than you have been. But now it ends."

He lifted his pistol and aimed it at her face. She ducked at once, pushed forward, shoving her shoulder into his belly, staggering him and making him stumble backward.

She had slipped away from the house shortly after Joseph had left, reasoning that she would be expected to be inside the house by any antagonists who might reach her. Now she ran toward the house, fighting panic, wishing she had never left it because in the house, at least, there were other weapons.

He ran after her, firing a shot that sang past her ear. The next shot hit her, clipping the edge of her heel through the miner's boots she wore. It was not a serious wound in itself, but it brought her down. He was upon her in a moment, raising the pistol and aiming it at her back.

She rolled quickly, making him delay firing, and kicked upward, hitting him in the knee. He stumbled sideways. She rose, elbowed him in the jaw, and ran as best she could toward the house.

He shot at her again, but the bullet missed her by an inch. She darted through the door and slammed it shut behind her, dropping its bar in place.

She turned, scared beyond words, and looked for a weapon. She ran to the rifle rack, but fumbled and dropped the only rifle there, then found it unloaded when she picked it up and checked it.

Coldwell rammed the door, rattling its hinges and making the locking bar strain. She heard him curse, then he hit the door again, hard enough almost to knock the bar out of place.

April turned and saw the Colonel's still form, sitting bizarrely, absurdly at the table, pistol in hand.

Coldwell rammed the door a third time, and fired a shot through it. April let out a little yell and went for the loaded pistol in the Colonel's hand.

The dead fingers gripped hard, however, and she did not succeed in pulling the pistol free. A second try and all she did was accidentally push back the hammer, which clicked into full cock.

The door gave way and burst open. April screamed and lurched away, seeking cover. Her motion bumped the body of the corpse at the table, tilting it to the edge of its chair.

Coldwell entered the room, pistol raised, and was stunned to see a man seated at the table, pistol in hand. Even more stunned was he when he saw the leathery face and, despite the distortion of death and mummification, recognized the visage of Colonel Bishop, the first man he had ever killed.

Coldwell froze, stunned and confused. The Colonel, already overbalanced, fell stiffly off the chair. The pistol discharged when the corpse hit the floor.

Coldwell let out a grunt and looked down at his chest, watching the fountain of blood that suddenly burst from him. He stared at it as if he couldn't believe it was there, then looked once again at the Colonel, and up at April.

"But . . . I killed him . . . myself. He can't have done this . . . he's dead."

"So are you, murderer!" she said. April dived for the floor, wrenched the pistol out of the Colonel's hand, and fired off two more quick shots, one hitting Coldwell in the belly, the other in the neck.

He fell, limp and loose, and died with the dead and empty eyes of the Colonel staring at him, the dead mouth drawn back into a hideous and brittle grin.

April dropped the pistol, came to her feet, and stumbled past the bodies of the long-dead Colonel Bishop and the freshly dead Hank Coldwell. Outdoors, she fell to her knees and was sick on the ground.

She remained in that posture a minute or so, then rose and went to the well, weeping, gasping, but sensing at the same time that the terror was over.

She drew up a bucket and splashed water on her face, cleaning herself, rinsing her mouth. Cooling the feverlike heat that had taken hold of her. Then she sank to the ground and leaned against the cool stone of the well wall.

She heard them coming and looked up slowly.

There was her uncle Michael, expression full of worry, lurching toward her, and behind him the two Carrigan brothers . . . and a third man, wonderfully familiar and welcome. But he was a dream, just a fantasy, for Patrick Carrigan was dead and gone, killed out on the Missouri plains.

But as she stared at the approaching phantom, he did not vanish as phantoms should. He reached her and knelt, looked into her face, and smiled at her.

"April," he said. "My dear April."

Her vision of him blurred, distorted by tears. She put her hand out and touched him, and knew then that he was indeed real, and alive, and back with her again. She embraced him, embracing the impossible without questioning it, then wept as she was overwhelmed by the deepest relief and purest joy she had known in a short and difficult life.

25

Michael McCree shook his head. "I still don't see it. No cause for you to leave that I can figure."

"It's for the best," Joseph said. "Those two are together again, and they don't need two Irish brothers hanging about the place, crowding them. Besides, I don't think the Colonel likes Liam very much." He winked.

"Pshaw! The Colonel thinks highly of both of you, companions! And I got to say, I'm proud of the Colonel. He got himself some vengeance, didn't he! Old Coldwell's probably the only gunslinger ever shot to death by a man he killed probably twenty years ago."

"There's a tale to tell the grandchildren," Liam said.

"Winter's coming on," McCree said. "I wish you'd stay."

"Winter coming on is one reason we need to go.

We need to get out of the mountains while we can and get back on our way."

"And find Patrick's father."

"Yep," Liam threw in. "And now I feel sure we can. He's told us where he is, and a lot about him. I feel like I'm going to see my father again, based on what Patrick describes."

"Did he say why they fell out with one another?"

"No. But he wants to mend the fences. He gave us this to pass on to his father when we see him." Liam pulled a sealed envelope from his pocket.

"What's it say?"

"I don't know. We'll not read it. It's private between father and son."

"April will miss you. She cried when I told her you were leaving."

"Tell her we'll see her again. We'll want to see that baby."

"You've got no horses now, and you've spent your money on supplies for us."

"We've taken enough to last us for a while. If we have to, we'll find work somewhere for a few days and make a few dollars. There's always a way."

He nodded, eyes twinkling. "That's right. Sometimes help comes from surprising places. When are you leaving?"

"First light tomorrow."

• • •

As April slept elsewhere in the cabin, Liam and Joseph talked to their cousin that night at length, coming to know him and see in him much of themselves. The manner of his speech was much like Liam's; his way of moving and smiling and holding himself were Joseph all over again. Family was an astonishing thing to two brothers who had enjoyed too little of it in their time.

"Are you certain that it's over?" Liam asked Patrick. "No chance at all of Maxwell finding himself another Coldwell and coming after you and April?"

"Believe me, it won't happen," Patrick said. "That's one thing you can be fully assured about. He'll never come after us. You may see some stories about him in the newspapers when you get down out of these mountains."

"He's dead?"

"Inexplicably missing."

"Is this one of those situations in which it's best not to know too much?" Joseph asked.

"Indeed it is, and I'll say no more about it. Joseph, how are the fingers?"

Joseph held up his left hand and wriggled it. "Still a little stiff, but not much pain. I'm glad to be out of the splints."

"A whole lot has happened since you hurt those fingers."

"If that train hadn't derailed, we'd never have been

in Culpepperville at the right time for April to find Liam. If I hadn't caught a glimpse of your sign about to be burned, I'd never have known you existed. And if Coldwell hadn't been careless in how he shot you out on the plains, you *wouldn't* have existed."

"The point Joseph is trying to make is one he makes all the time. He's obsessed with it, matter of fact. He believes that everything happens for a reason, that every bird fluttering by is trying to send him a message or give him a portent. Sometimes I think he's an Indian instead of an Irishman."

"You don't believe those things, eh?"

"Sometimes I believe things just happen, no particular reason or meaning. Sometimes I'm not so sure."

They saw April one final time before they left. She visited them briefly, kissing each of them, thanking them for all they had done for her. Even Liam teared up a little. She went away after that, unwilling actually to witness their departure.

"You know, Joseph, I could have truly loved that woman," Liam said. "I believe I could have spent my life with her. And I don't care that she had a baby by another man. I could overlook all that and be a fine and devoted husband to her."

"You would have had a problem with that, Liam. She'd be too much in love with your brother for it ever to work out between you."

"My brother flatters himself."

"The end of it all is that it doesn't really matter. It's Patrick who has her, heart and soul, and I think that's how it's supposed to be."

"I can't deny it. But it's going to take me a good while to quit thinking about her all the time."

"Me too. But it's been quite an adventure, huh? Who'd have ever thought it! Look back over the past year, Liam. We've gone bust in the worst cattle drive ever undertaken, nearly gotten ourselves killed in Dodge City, built barns in Missouri, and shot it out with a gang of hired killers in a mining camp ghost town in Colorado. You can't say we haven't had things to occupy us."

"Maybe things will be more peaceful from here on out."

"You never know. It all depends on what's meant to be."

"Or what just chances to happen."

"Either way, there's one thing I can predict with certainty: We're destined to look for work right away. As Michael McCree would say, we're about broke, companion."

Liam grinned. "Michael McCree and I had a talk this morning in private. He said, 'Liam, I'm going to let you in on a secret. Everybody left this mining camp because they believed it was played out. It ain't. I've hit a strike that makes the original one look very small.'"

"McCree said that?"

"Yep."

"He was pulling your leg, then. That man lives in poverty. If he had a strike, he'd not have let us spend almost every cent we have on supplies for the winter. He'd have bought them himself."

"He never intended that we'd actually be the ones buying them," Liam said. "He planned to reimburse us for every cent . . . after spending enough time around us for him to see whether we could be trusted to keep his secret."

"But he never repaid us."

"He did. More than repaid." Liam produced a small cloth bag and tossed it to Joseph. It was so heavy Joseph almost dropped it as he caught it.

"You've got to be joshing me."

"Nope. When we cash that in we'll be better fixed than we've been in a year. It makes me inclined to stop down in Brasstown and have a drink or two before we go on our way. Just to celebrate being alive, you know."

Joseph grinned. "I can go along with that. Come on, Liam. Let's walk faster. You're plodding along slower than old Ben."

They sped their pace and headed toward Brasstown as the sun rose higher above them, bathing the mountains with a pure and crystalline light.

Visit
❖ **Pocket Books** ❖
online at

www.SimonSays.com

Keep up on the latest new
releases from your favorite
authors, as well as author
appearances, news, chats,
special offers and more.